Desert Heat

Jamie DeBree

Thank you for your purchase. For a free digital
copy of *Desert Heat*, please visit
BrazenSnakeBooks.com.

Desert Heat
ISBN 0983198802
EAN-13 9780983198802
Desert Heat Copyright © 2010 Jamie M DeBree
Published by Brazen Snake Books

Edited by India Drummond
Cover art by Heidi Sutherlin

For Carol, Erica, Heidi, and Brooklyn –
I'm honored to call you friends.

Also by the Author

Tempest

Chapter One

Marie fidgeted with the low scoop-collar of her cocktail dress as she eavesdropped on the dean of the science department and the college president. The two men were blithely plotting her downfall while she hid behind a large fake ficus tree.

"Some research just has to be cut. Enrollment is down and we simply don't have the money to fund outside projects." Tom Cranston, head of the university, didn't sound all that upset to Marie. He was not a fan of pharmaceutical research anyway, and even though the company she worked for provided ample compensation for anything created in the college lab, the money apparently wasn't enough.

"Yes, but in this case, I think you'd be making a grave error to cut Dr. Simco's funding instead of Adams'." Marie grinned at the comment from Emery Williams, head of the science department and one of her staunchest advocates. "Adams has done his time - his ideas are getting stale. Simco has fresh new thinking and research to bring to the table. I wouldn't dismiss her out of hand."

Marie glanced through silk leaves at the milling crowd. Riley Adams, the other subject of the debate, was standing by the buffet munching on shrimp and drinking a mixed drink from two colored straws. He had been a professor for fifteen years, and Marie had taken many of his classes as an undergrad. She respected his abilities and had always considered him one of the best instructors she'd had. It didn't hurt that he was easy to look at as well, very distinguished with a trim frame and dark hair and eyes.

It was disconcerting that he was her rival now, but that didn't mean she would step aside. He'd built a solid name for himself, and he could undoubtedly get funding somewhere else if the college didn't come through. Just starting out in her career, Marie needed all the help she could get to continue her research on natural pharmaceuticals. She was confident that someday it would revolutionize medicine. Hearing her name, she tuned back into the conversation on the other side of the tree.

"Just give Simco a chance," Emery was saying. "Give her a deadline. Better yet, give them both a deadline - say two months - to publish something spectacular. Whoever publishes first wins the grant." Marie frowned. None of her projects could possibly be publishable in the next two months. It wasn't enough time to turn raw data into fully-tested and ready-to-announce findings.

Cranston laughed. "Okay Williams - you've got a deal. But it's six-weeks. I want original, publishable papers on my desk within six weeks, and the subject with the most potential wins the grant. Will that work?"

"Fine," Emery said. Marie's mouth rounded in silent shock. How could she possibly have something ready to publish in six weeks? No one ever did that. At least she didn't think they did. She looked at Riley again, who had moved on from shrimp and found the brownie plate.

"Shall I tell them, or do you want to?" Williams sounded perturbed.

"I'll tell them tomorrow." Emery moved away from the tree, and Williams followed, their voices fading as they rejoined the other partiers.

Marie took a sip of wine, wishing she could stay hidden. Introverted to the core, she didn't like other people well enough to suffer through the whole small talk rigmarole. But if her funding was in trouble, it would be a good idea to have a backup source. Recognizing a couple of investors from her last major project standing by the bar, she decided to go re-introduce herself, maybe get their business cards. Perhaps they'd have a job available if she lost this ridiculous game.

Glancing down to make sure she wasn't too rumpled, she stepped out from behind the tree and stopped short as she hit something tall and unyielding. Struggling for balance, she found herself braced against a very broad, hard chest that had to be the result of intense physical training. Large hands settled at her hips just long enough to steady her on the ridiculous spike heels that Cynthia, her lab assistant, had insisted she wear.

His touch set off a wild chain of tingling nerves that traveled throughout her body, finally settling between her legs in a surge of warmth. Shifting, she took one step back, her eyes still on the tight button-down shirt. She'd just about pay money to see what was underneath.

"Are you okay?"

Marie froze at the deep, velvety voice. She'd heard it before, but where? Her brows drew together as she looked up into the emerald eyes of Darren Newbury, Riley's main assistant. Great. She nodded, resisting the urge to pet his chest with her fingers. He was one of the few men she'd ever thought of as "pretty", though she was fairly certain he'd be offended at the description. Ever since they'd taken classes together, she'd had a bit of a crush on him. Her brain never seemed to work right around good-looking men, and she inevitably said something painfully stupid. Deciding early on that she'd rather admire from afar than look like an idiot, she went out of her way to avoid interacting with any man who made her drool, including this one.

"Dr. Simco?" He raised one brow, and she swallowed hard. It was happening again, just like it always did. This was her cue to say something stupid that would send him running the other way. Just like every other hunk she'd ever met.

"I'm...uh...good, fine," she sputtered. "I was just going to talk to some colleagues over by the bar," she said, gesturing toward the other side of the room with one hand. Unfortunately, it was the hand that held her wine glass, and the dark liquid sloshed out, spots appearing as if by magic on Darren's bright white dress shirt. At least his jacket was black. She stared, trying to think of something, anything, to say that would make it okay.

"I'm so sorry," she said, avoiding his eyes. A waiter passed by, and she tapped him on the shoulder. "Do you happen to have a napkin?" He nodded, handing her several from his tray. She patted at Darren's shirt and managed only to make the stain wider.

"It's okay," he said, chuckling as he closed one hand over hers and took the napkins with the other. All coherent thought fled at his touch, and she froze as he leaned closer. He smiled, lowering his head until his face was just inches from hers.

"Do you want to know a secret?" he murmured.

She blinked, stunned, as if he'd asked her to solve a complex math equation. "Umm..."

"This shirt has a hole in the side. I didn't have time to change into a fresh one, so I haven't been able to take my jacket off all night. I was planning to throw it away as soon as I got home anyway. The shirt, not the jacket." He straightened with a wink and buttoned his blazer, covering the worst of the splotch.

"Oh," Marie said, still flustered from being so close to him. "I, uh, guess that's okay then." Not sure what to say next, she turned away. "I'll just go find Dr. Adams now." She dared to glance up at him one more time and saw confusion in his eyes, along with the look that said he'd just realized she was eccentric, and not in a good way.

Face burning, she made her way to the coat check, stopping only to leave her wineglass on the bar. She'd heard - and done - enough for one night. It was time to retreat to the sterile comfort of her lab and try to figure out how to win her funding for the next year.

* * *

After the official announcement the next morning, Marie rifled through a stack of folders. Her current project had recently hit a dead end, and she couldn't find anything that could be condensed into the six-week time frame of the contest. One of the local drug companies had a couple of other things they wanted her to work on, but neither looked very interesting, and she'd been avoiding them because they involved synthetic drugs. She preferred to work with natural substances whenever possible.

Maybe she should have taken the job Merrill Pharmaceuticals had offered six months ago. It was good pay, and once she'd completed a few projects she would have been able to put in a good word or two for more natural materials and research. She stared out the window, confused and frustrated.

A knock at the door startled her. Cynthia, her lab assistant poked her head around the frame.

"Got a minute?"

Marie waved her in. "Sure, what's up?"

"I have something I think you might want to take a look at," she said, passing some papers across the desk and then taking a seat in one of the chairs across from Marie. "We need something spectacular to get our funding this year, right?"

Marie nodded, scanning over the first page with a frown.

"Read the article on the second page, half-way down. It's a risk, but if it paid off, we'd get all the funding we need, and probably whatever else we want. Don't you think?" Marie glanced up, smiling briefly at her assistant before finding the article. Cynthia always wanted her to start a study on some ancient herbal remedy for this or that, but never had enough evidence for Marie to justify spending her precious budget on a long-shot. She read through the article. It claimed that a hard-to-find flowering plant called the Mawai that only grew in the New Mexico desert held the cure to viruses such as the flu. She finished the short paragraph and then looked up. Cynthia was nibbling at her fingernails.

"I know what you're going to say," she said, before Marie could comment. "You're going to tell me there's not enough evidence, and that even if there was, it's not important enough to sell any of the big companies on. So we can't afford to waste our money chasing after a long-shot."

Marie smiled, setting the paper back on the desk. "And you're going to tell me I'm wrong, that all the major drug companies will be fighting over this particular cure, and that we can't win big if we don't take risks."

"It's all true, you know." Cynthia leaned forward, bracing her hands on the edge of the desk. "But one thing is different this time."

"What's that?"

"This time, you can't afford not to take the risk." She paused, letting that sink in. "If we don't try, we stand to lose everything. Unless you have some other idea that will blow the socks off the funding committee, we don't have a chance at beating Riley. If we do go after this, and nothing happens, you still lose everything."

"So why would I want to do this again?" Marie propped one elbow on the desk and rested her chin on the heel of her hand. In spite of her reservations, she found herself intrigued. A cure for the flu? What would that mean to society as a whole?

Cynthia grinned. "Because if it does turn out that this plant can naturally cure the flu virus, we go to the media first, instead of the drug guys. Everyone in the world wants a cure for the flu, Marie - once the general public finds out there is one, and that it's natural, they'll insist on getting it. Bidding wars will ensue, we'll be rich, you'll be famous, and the money will flow like water for your next project." She laughed, sitting back in the chair with a smug expression on her face.

Marie picked up the paper, and scanned the article again. The original recipe for the cure had been handed down by word of mouth for years, maybe even centuries, by the natives in the area. Local opinions were divided, and with the recent mutations of the virus going around interest had risen again, though nothing the scientific community would ever take seriously. Most researchers focused on creating cures, not finding them, which was why it was so hard for Marie to get her work noticed. Something like this could make her career soar.

On the other hand, it could just as easily send it careening into the nearest tree if nothing came of it. She sighed, closing her eyes and rubbing the bridge of her nose. It was now or never, but did she dare? Taking a deep breath, Marie opened her eyes. Cynthia was biting her nails again, watching her intently.

"Okay," Marie said, regretting the word almost immediately. "Get a plan written up for the trip. We'll have to work fast, since we have six-weeks to do all the testing and present our findings to the dean. I'll get a team together - we're going to need some help. Can you be ready by Friday?"

Cynthia stood, smiling as she walked to the door. "Absolutely. This is going to be the best thing we've ever done. You'll see." She disappeared into the hall and Marie turned to the computer, preparing to compose a list of prospective team members.

"I hope so," she murmured, opening a new document on the screen.

* * *

A tap on his shoulder startled Darren, and he bit back a curse as the knife he was holding barely missed his finger. He turned to glare at the offender and found Cynthia Newman, Dr. Simco's lab assistant, grinning widely at him.

"You'll never guess what project we're going to take on for the competition," she whispered, leaning in. Darren glanced around the lab, locating his boss at desk several feet away.

He stood, motioning for her to follow and led the way to a storage room down the hall. "It must be something good - anything I can get in on?" He'd struck up a friendship with Cynthia soon after getting a job with Dr. Adams. He'd always wanted to work with Marie Simco, but every time he'd tried to approach her to discuss his rejected application, she'd avoided him. He probably shouldn't have accepted Cynthia's help, but she was clearly attracted to him. Not wanting to alienate her and her boss in turn, he took advantage of her interest. She kept him apprised of Simco's current projects, and Darren was just waiting for the right time to offer his services in hopes of getting a spot on her team.

Of course, the fact that Dr. Simco was very attractive didn't help. Last night it had seemed like he was finally getting somewhere with her. Too bad she hadn't stuck around just a little longer.

"We're going to find the cure for the flu," she announced, waving a folder at him. "There's a flower in New Mexico with compounds that supposedly kill the virus. We're going to find it, and develop a cure. Not a vaccine, a real, honest-to-goodness cure."

Darren looked through the file, noting the accelerated time table. "So you're leaving on Friday?"

"Yep. But it gets better." She paused. "She needs a research team. I was thinking I'd recommend you...if you're interested."

Darren looked up, and Cynthia waggled her eyebrows at him. "Do you think she'll go for it - me, I mean?"

"Never know until you try. But I have a feeling not too many people are going to jump at this one, it being such a risk and all. You should think about that too," she said, tilting her head. Her smile faded.

"There's a good chance that anyone associated with this will have to start over at the bottom if it fails. Are you okay with that?"

Darren didn't hesitate. "Yes," he said, handing the file back to her. "I believe in your boss's work. If she thinks this is worth running with, that's all I need. When should I talk to her?"

"Let me bring it up first. I'll do it now and get back to you, okay?"

Darren nodded, opening the door and preceding her into the hall. His friendship with Cynthia had finally paid off. He locked it again once she was out, and went back to the lab to wait. He could hardly focus when he sat back down in front of his slides, thinking about the shy Dr. Simco, and the shirt he hadn't thrown out after all.

* * *

Cynthia knocked on the door just as Marie was ready to give up. There was only room in the budget for two people aside from her normal crew of three. She absolutely had to have at least one more technician to run the tests as fast as possible, plus a photographer to document the plant, the compounds and the environment. There were only a couple of techs in the department that might be able to handle the pace, but unfortunately, they both worked for Riley Adams. And all the normal department photographers were either on assignment or balking at the quick departure date. Mid-terms were next week, and most of the photographers were students who helped out for extra cash. She rubbed her temples, motioning for Cynthia to come in.

"I hope you have good news," she said, looking pointedly at the folder in Cynthia's hands. "I'm getting nowhere with the extra team members we need."

Cynthia opened the folder, and handed over a sheet of paper. "Well, I've got the itinerary done. Depending on how long it takes us to find the plant, I think we can make the deadline, as long as we have another tech to help determine whether further research and testing will be viable. We need someone who can work fast, and knows what he's doing..."

"I take it you have someone in mind?" Marie raised her eyebrows and folded her arms over her chest.

Cynthia nodded. "Actually, I do. Darren Newbury would be perfect." Marie shook her head. No way would she hire someone from Dr. Adams' team. What if they reported back to him on her research, and he published it as his own? What if he paid them to sabotage her? She opened her mouth to protest, but her assistant was too quick.

"He's wanted to work with you ever since he started here, Marie."

Marie frowned. Why would someone like him want to work with her? And if that was the case, why hadn't he ever applied to her part of the lab?

"He applied when he first started here, but you turned him down flat. He assumed it was because he was male, but didn't want to push you. He'd really like the chance to work with you on this, to leave Adams' team and go on the expedition. I think you should give him a shot." Cynthia sat down, fingering the edge of the manila folder..

Marie leaned back in her chair, remembering. It had been several years earlier. Darren was right - she had turned him down because of his gender, or rather the way he made her want things she shouldn't. If anyone ever found out, she'd be fired for sure. She'd been tongue-tied the entire interview, unable to do or say anything aside from what she'd scripted, because just being near him made her tense up and forget the most basic things. Like spelling her own name. She'd been positive that working with him would be impossible, and her work would suffer. That was why she'd declined to offer him the job, even though he was easily the most talented tech who'd applied. Instead, she'd hired Nell Carson, a no-nonsense woman who just wanted to study holistic medicine.

"Did you turn him down because he's male?" Cynthia's voice pulled her out of her musing. "People notice that you only hire women, you know. It would do your reputation some good to have a man on the team. I mean, it's discrimination to not hire someone based on what sex they are, right?"

So that was how this was going to play out. There

was no way to win this without a potential lawsuit. "Okay," she said, holding her hands up in surrender. "You win. Tell Newbury he's got the job if he wants it. If you can find me a photographer while you're at it, I'll buy you dinner."

"I was actually hoping I could buy you dinner, Dr. Simco." Marie looked up to see the subject of their conversation standing in the doorway, one broad shoulder leaning casually against the frame. He had the grace to look contrite, but Marie was still annoyed.

"Dr. Newbury - do you make a habit of listening in on other people's conversations?" she asked, wishing she sounded sterner. At least her voice didn't shake like her insides at the moment. God, the man was beautiful.

He shrugged, flashing an apologetic grin. "Sorry. I came to see if I could help Cynthia plead my case, but it sounds like she did fine by herself." His grin faded, green eyes turning an intense stare on her. "I want you to know though - I would never have filed suit against you. If you prefer women on your team, that's fine with me. But I'm honored you've agreed to let me be part of your research." He straightened and Marie stood, intimidated by his six-foot-something frame. She held out her hand, determined to be professional about the arrangement. Warmth infused her skin as he squeezed her fingers gently.

"Welcome to the team, Dr. Newbury. Cynthia will

keep you informed as to the itinerary and travel arrangements. When will you be giving Dr. Adams notice?" She noted Cynthia still sitting in her chair, an odd look on her face as she watched them.

"I quit before I came over," he said, his smile back in place. "It was fun, actually - his face got all red and he called me a traitor." He chuckled, and Marie glanced over to Cynthia, who was smiling. "So, dinner everyone?"

Marie shook her head. "I'll pass. But thank you for the offer. If you could be here at nine tomorrow morning, we'll discuss everything we need to take on the trip as well as basic personal supplies. I'll see you then." She turned and walked back behind her desk, not expecting him to still be standing there after she'd clearly dismissed him. "Was there something else?"

Cynthia stood up, flashing Marie a disgusted look as she turned to smile at Darren. "Come on Darren, I'll show you around, and you can buy me dinner. Dr. Simco has a hard time with new people." She winked at Marie and took Darren's arm, propelling him out of the office.

Marie sighed, shaking her head. She turned back to the computer, wondering how they'd be ready to go in four days. And how she'd get through the whole trip with that hunky lab tech distracting her at every turn.

Chapter Two

When Marie arrived at the airport, Dr. Nell Carson, the other full-time member of her team met her at the door. "There's a problem with the flight," Nell said, taking one of the huge equipment bags out of Marie's hands. "Our plane is delayed, and according to the time table, that means we'll miss our connecting flight from Denver to New Mexico. We'll have to stay overnight in Denver."

Marie tried to think through the fog in her still-sleeping brain. "Are there any other--"

Just then, Cynthia came through the doors with Darren and a tall, slender man Marie assumed was the photographer. Nell waved them over as Marie studied the tickets.

"Is there a problem?" Darren asked. His voice sent her nerves into overdrive and adrenaline rushing through her system.

"Uh...just a scheduling mix-up," Marie mumbled, picking up her bags again. "I was just going to the counter to check these and get more information."

She turned, hoping no one had noticed the flush in her cheeks. Behind her, bags rustled and shoes clacked against the white tile floor as her new team followed.

Half an hour later, they were through security and heading to the gate. The clerk hadn't been able to help them – apparently this was the only flight to Denver for several hours, so they'd have to wait. Marie tried to sit and relax, but flying always made her nervous. She got up and paced in front of the huge windows overlooking the tarmac. The trip starting this way seemed like a bad omen. Worse, the coffee shop wasn't open yet, so even the comfort of warm stimulants in a cup to soothe her nerves was out of her control.

"Dr. Simco?"

Marie stopped, turning away from the windows to find her assistant smiling at her, the tall man by her side.

"This is Scott Ellis - our photographer for the project. Scott, meet Dr. Marie Simco, our team leader."

He held out his hand, and Marie took it, noting part of a tattoo peeking out from under the cuff of his leather jacket. He had a strong grip, but not too strong, and she appreciated that he didn't try to crush her hand like so many men. His face was long, with angular lines that weren't exactly handsome, but attractive all the same. Dark brown eyes regarded her with warmth - and maybe a hint of interest?

"Nice to meet you, Mr. Ellis. Thanks for coming on such short notice." She took her hand back, giving him what she hoped was a friendly smile.

He inclined his head in a deferential nod. "Please, call me Scott. Nice to meet you, too. I hear we're headed to the desert? I'm looking forward to warmer weather."

Marie nodded. "The days should be pleasantly warm this time of year, but the nights will be cold. I hope you brought clothing for a broad range of temperatures." She noticed the others watching with interest. "Let me introduce you to the lab techs."

She gestured to the petite redhead first. "This is Dr. Nell Carson. She's been working with me for three years now. She's in charge of the equipment, and will let you know what we need for photos of the actual work."

Nell's lips turned up slightly and she half-waved in a manner of greeting. Marie turned to Darren, who stood.

"And this is Dr. Darren Newbury, a tech we've hired for this project. If Nell or Cynthia can't answer your questions, he should be able to." Darren shook Scott's hand, and Marie stifled a frown as she noted both men's arms tense, as though considerable pressure was being exerted. A classic male dominance tactic, she was curious whether Cynthia or Nell had triggered it. She'd have to watch carefully and make sure the instinctive competition or any resulting relationships didn't affect the project.

A loud clattering in the hallway made her jump, her surprise subsiding quickly as she realized the coffee shop had just opened. "Coffee, anyone?"

Not waiting for an answer, she brushed between the two men and towards the intoxicating scent of freshly ground beans.

* * *

Darren let out a deep breath when he finally entered his hotel room several hours later. It had been a long flight to Denver, between listening to a yowling cat who apparently did not appreciate being up in the clouds, and watching the photographer flirt with Marie the whole way. How had he gotten a seat right next to her anyway? He tossed his bag on the bed and took out the manila folder containing the project's specifics. He sat on the bed, his back propped against the headboard, and started reading.

He'd gotten halfway through the file when the phone beside him rang. He hesitated a moment and then picked it up.

"Hello?"

"Darren, it's Nell." He opened his mouth to reply, but she didn't pause. "Do you happen to have your copy of the itinerary handy? Dr. Simco left hers back at the lab, and she's trying to decide how we can make up for this lost time when we get to New Mexico."

He flipped to the front of the folder, finding the page she needed. "I have it right here," he said, getting to his feet. "What room is she in? I'll take it to her." He tried to ignore the fact that his pulse sped up at the thought of being alone with her, even for a few minutes.

"Room two-fifteen," Nell said. She seemed preoccupied, and he wondered what she was doing - or trying to do - while talking to him. In his experience, most women couldn't focus on just one thing. He shook his head. At least Marie's room was on this floor - only a couple doors down the hall.

"Uh...okay. Thanks - I'll talk to you later."

Darren stared at the phone as the connection went silent. He wondered what Marie was doing. Working, probably. She didn't seem like the type to relax very often.

He put the phone down and got the plastic room key off the table. He considered putting his shoes on, but couldn't bear the thought of putting his feet back into them. He padded into the hall, surprised to find room two-fifteen right across the hall from his. He crossed the bold, flowery carpet to her door and knocked, surprised when she opened the door almost immediately.

"Nell told me you were coming." Her eyes moved over his body and he fought the urge to squirm under her scrutiny. An old t-shirt hanging loose over old jeans that just grazed the top of his bare feet wasn't exactly work attire. She looked up again, and met his gaze with one eyebrow arched. "Comfortable?"

He grinned, glancing at his feet, and noting that her own were bare too, with surprisingly bright shade of pink polish on her toenails. "Getting there, anyway." He looked her over too, taking his time to examine every detail. He'd never seen her hair down before; she always wore it up at work. It swirled around her face and shoulders in gentle waves, the red highlights shimmering through dark brown in the lamp light. The business jacket she'd worn buttoned up all day was gone, with only a thin yellow t-shirt covering her ample breasts. Wishing he had x-ray vision, he noticed her chest moving a little faster as she breathed. Could he be affecting her as much as she affected him?

Ever since the party, he'd wondered if she felt the chemistry building between them. When he'd leaned over to speak to her, it had felt like a magnet was pulling him in. Unable to resist testing the theory, he took a step forward. Then another. He felt a definite connection the moment he crossed into her personal space.

"Um...did you bring the schedule, Dar...uh...Dr. Newbury?" There was something in her tone that Darren couldn't quite describe. Panic? Desire, maybe? He looked into her eyes as he held the document up. Definitely desire, he noted before she looked away and reached for the page.

"You feel it too, don't you?" Mentally, he cursed himself for saying it aloud. Even if it was true, he knew she was scared. He saw it in her tense muscles, and the set of her jaw. Would she kick him off the team? He reached out a hand, ran a single finger over her collarbone. She shivered.

"I...um...don't think..."

He slid his finger up to her neck, her pulse strong and fast under his touch. "Good," he said. Had she swayed closer? "Don't think. Close your eyes. Feel."

Her lashes fluttered down, and he nearly groaned. She was so beautiful. He caressed a path down her chest and up the center of her throat to trace along her jaw. Lacing his fingers in her hair he cupped her head, coaxing it back as he stepped up to press his body against hers. She was so warm, melting into his chest as he leaned over and kissed her neck, her jaw, her lips.

She whimpered, hesitating a moment before letting him in, kissing him back with a hunger that seemed contrary to her controlling nature. She wrapped her arms around his neck, and he pulled her more tightly against him, backing her into the room and letting the door swing shut. He slid his hands down to cup her buttocks, his arousal pressing hard against the front of her jeans. He laved once more at her lips and then kissed down the side of her neck, bending her backward enough that he could taste the smooth place between her breasts.

Three loud thumps came from behind him, and he glanced over his shoulder with a frown. Marie was struggling in his arms, and he turned back to her, noting the bright red color rising in her cheeks and her refusal to look in his eyes. He let her go, careful to make sure she was steady before removing his hands from her arms.

"Oh my god," she said, turning away from him and running a hand through her hair. "That's probably Scott. What was I thinking?" She turned back, distress lining her face. "I'm so sorry. That was a huge mistake. You have to go."

Darren frowned. "What's wrong?" He picked up the forgotten itinerary, holding it out to her. She grabbed it, laying it on the table, and twisted her hair into the tidy style she always wore, securing it with a few pins. She spared him only a cursory glance, her normal bland expression back in place.

"I'm having dinner with Scott," she said, reaching for her jacket and buttoning it back over her shirt. He realized the wanton woman he'd just been with was gone, and the cool, controlled doctor was back. "We made plans on the plane." Three more knocks sounded, and Darren felt like opening the door and punching the man on the other side.

"Cancel," he said, blocking her way as she walked briskly toward the door. "Stay with me."

A flicker of that other woman sparked briefly in her eyes when she finally met his gaze. "I can't." She looked down, staring at his chest. "I'm sorry - you're just too...too...you." She brushed past him and pulled the door open. Darren turned, feeling only marginally better when he saw the questions on the photographer's face.

"I'll be ready in just a moment," Marie said, glancing at Darren with a professional smile. "Dr. Newbury just stopped by to replace my copy of the schedule, and we were going over a few things." She reached for the black clutch sitting on the bathroom counter and tucked it under her arm. "Have a good evening."

Barely managing to keep his fingers from curling into fists, he moved past her and nodded to the other man. "Have a good evening," he managed, stalking across the hall to his room. The other door slammed shut, and he imagined them walking together down the hall as he started stripping off his clothes. First, a cold shower. Then maybe he'd be able to think clearly enough to figure out what was so wrong with being him.

*** * ***

Marie kept her expression casual as Darren went into the room right across the hall from hers. Knowing he'd be there when she got back - just a few steps away while she slept - made her cheeks heat all over again. She flashed what she hoped was a normal smile at Scott.

"Ready to go?"

She could tell he was curious, but he just nodded. "Whenever you are." He held out his elbow and after a moment's hesitation she slipped her hand through, resting her fingers on his arm. She walked by his side to the elevators, feeling awkward being so close. She was relieved when he released her as the doors closed behind them.

When they reached the lobby, he put a hand at the small of her back, steering her toward the fancy restaurant situated in a corner near a darkened jewelry store. She waited for that tingle of awareness to come where he touched her, but only felt comfortable warmth. Once they were seated, he ordered a beer. She ordered water, earning a questioning look.

"I don't drink often," she said, used to explaining. "I like to stay in control." She shrugged.

He tilted his head to the side. "Really?" He took a long swig of his beer. "Have you ever been drunk?"

She nodded, staring at her water glass. "Just once, in college." She took a sip. "It...uh, didn't end well."

"Ah." He reached across the table to put a hand over hers. "Sorry to hear that."

She looked into his eyes and saw that he was sincere. Smiling again, she retrieved her hand and picked up her menu. "So, what do you think is good here?"

He chuckled. "Steak's good anywhere - that's what I always have."

"I should have guessed you'd say that," she said,

studying the offerings. "I think I'll have the lasagna." The waiter came back and they placed their orders.

"So what are we looking for? Cynthia said it's some kind of natural cure."

Marie nodded, grateful for a familiar subject. "It's a plant the natives say can cure the flu virus. With all the new mutations lately, everyone is scared of getting sick. And I need a big find to secure funding for my lab. If this works out, it should solve all my problems."

"And if it doesn't?"

She shrugged. "I lose everything."

The waiter brought their food and fresh drinks. Scott raised his beer for a toast. "To curing the flu and a long career." She clinked her glass with his, hoping to feel that spark of attraction. Mildly disappointed when she didn't, she merely inclined her head in thanks, and tucked into her dinner. Scott seemed like a normal, stable guy, and he didn't intimidate her with his average looks. It was really too bad he wasn't triggering her endorphins.

He walked her to her room afterwards, and she fitted her key card in the electronic lock, nudging the door open just a little.

"Thank you for dinner," she said, smiling up at him. "I had a good time."

He stepped a little closer. "Anytime." His grin wasn't just friendly, and even with her limited experience with men, she knew he was going to kiss her.

Her gaze drifted over his shoulder as he leaned in, glancing at the door across the hall. Would it be anything like Darren's kiss? She knew even as Scott's lips closed over hers that nothing would compare to whatever she'd experienced earlier. Realizing she was being kissed by one man while fantasizing about another, she closed her eyes and focused on the soft lips pressed chastely to her mouth.

Neither of them moved for a long moment, and when she finally pulled back, he brushed the fingers of one hand softly over the side of her face. "It's not going to happen, is it?"

Surprised and grateful at his candor, she let out a relieved breath. "I'm sorry. I don't think so." She gave him rueful grin. "Thank you for understanding."

He nodded, pulling her in for a casual hug. "You can't force something that isn't there." He glanced over his shoulder briefly. "Besides, I was pretty sure I felt some tension between you and the new lab tech..." His tone was teasing, and she laughed.

"I don't think so." She kept her eyes on Scott, rather than looking over at Darren's door again. "I can't talk to guys like that - they make me nervous." As soon as the words were out, she wished she could take them back. Why had she admitted that aloud?

He chuckled. "Guys like what? Smart guys? You're probably smarter than he is..."

"It has nothing to do with brains." She turned to her door, pushing it farther open. "Just forget I said anything, okay? I'll see you in the morning." She stepped inside and closed the door before he could press her with more questions. It had been a very long evening, and she flipped the security bar on the door, moving to her suitcase and pulled out an over-sized t-shirt to sleep in.

Ten minutes later, she was huddled in the too-hard hotel bed, shivering as she waited for the cold sheets to warm up. Closing her eyes, she imagined Darren lying next to her, those big, muscular arms wrapped tightly around her waist to chase the chill away.

* * *

Darren lay awake, one arm behind his head as he stared up at the ceiling. From what he'd seen through the peephole, Marie's date with Scott had gone well, but that kiss had looked pretty lackluster from his limited vantage point. It had taken every ounce of self-control not to open the door and knock the other guy out, dragging Marie back to his room like a cave man claiming his woman. She hadn't invited Scott in though, and she'd been looking at his door during that kiss.

Was that why she hadn't offered the photographer a nightcap? He grinned in the darkness at the thought that his touch, his kisses had spoiled her for the other man. As hot as it had been between them, how much better would it be to have her here with him now, lay-ing across his chest with her hair falling like silk across his skin. He would stroke her back with his fingertips, all the way down to her rounded buttocks where he'd squeeze gently. Her short, plain nails would rake down his ribs, sending shivers of awareness through his body, bringing his erection back to the ready. She'd take him in her hand, slowly moving up and down his shaft until he writhed in pleasure. He'd flip her on her back and drive urgently into her tight, wet core. She'd whimper underneath him, those little sounds that had driven him crazy earlier. Would she cry out when she came, or moan low in her throat? He groaned, palming himself under the covers. It didn't take long for his release, and he tossed the covers back, exhaling a ragged breath at the thought of sharing the next time with Marie.

He went into the bathroom and turned on the shower for the second time that night, stepping in to clean his body and hopefully clear his mind. But the nagging question remained - what held her back her from exploring the obvious chemistry between them? He soaped himself up, thinking about the classes they'd had together in college. What kind of guys had she dated back then? He frowned. Had she dated at all?

He put the soap down, letting the warm water sluice down his body. He didn't think she had been with anyone of note back then, or he would have remembered. Now that he thought about it, he couldn't remember anyone she'd dated since going to work at the lab either. He was certain she liked men - there's no way she could have faked her response to him - even if she was a bit cold with her date for the evening.

He got out, turned off the water and toweled himself dry. Turning to the mirror, he examined his features, comparing them to his rival. A little shorter even at a slightly over six feet, Scott had dark hair and somewhat average-looking features. The photographer wasn't overtly muscular, but probably strong, judging from how he walked.

Darren was taller by a few inches, and he stared intently at his face, trying to decide if a woman would find the angular lines and green eyes attractive. He couldn't resist flexing one of his biceps, noting the nicely sculpted ball that bulged when he pulled his fist toward his shoulder. Maybe she preferred her men smaller and less scruffy, he thought ruefully as he stroked the light stubble on his jaw line.

He got into bed, the cool sheets a welcome contrast after the hot shower. He wanted her. And based on her response to his touch, she wanted him too. He closed his eyes, pulling the covers to his neck. He'd just have to figure out what it was about him that she objected to and convince her it wasn't an issue.

Even if that meant a duel with the skinny photographer.

Chapter Three

The next morning, Marie took her seat on the plane to New Mexico and leaned against the headrest. Unable to sleep, she'd merely dozed on and off all night, finally getting up to an aching head and an incredibly bad mood. She prayed that whoever got the window seat next to her wouldn't want to chat. She intended to catch up on at least an hour's worth of sleep during the flight.

"Tired?"

The velvet voice that had haunted her most of the night sent warmth flooding through her body. The reaction irritated her, and when she looked up into his stunning eyes, it appeared as though he knew exactly what she was feeling.

"I never sleep well in hotels," she said, taking pride in the fact that her voice didn't shake. "Looking for your seat?"

He nodded, waving his ticket in her direction. "I think I just found it, actually." He gestured to the empty seat beside her.

"None of our tickets were together - how did you get a new seat assignment?" Unable to temper the annoyance in her tone, she looked away, grateful for the dark sunglasses she still wore. How could she keep her distance if he was right next to her the whole flight?

"They had to move us around because we missed last night's flight." He shrugged, easily stepping over her legs to slide into the small space. "Thank goodness this isn't a long flight. The human body isn't meant to be crammed into these small spaces for long." He stowed his laptop case under the seat in front of him and leaned back in his seat. "Do you want me to close the window shade?"

She shook her head, trying to ignore the fact that his arm was touching hers, sending tingles of awareness up her shoulder. "It's fine." She closed her eyes, his scent growing inexplicably stronger. "I'm just going to nap for a while, if you don't mind."

"Think I might do that too, actually."

She listened as he snapped the seat belt ends together, felt him shifting, his arm occasionally tapping hers. No matter how he moved, his left thigh pressed against her right. Heat radiated from his body, and it was irritating to realize that she wanted to move closer into his comfortable warmth.

She kept her arms crossed tightly over her chest and tried to ignore it when she felt him prop an arm on the armrest between them, establishing contact from shoulder to elbow in one small movement. The armrest folded up, she remembered, wondering how she'd react if he pushed it up and pulled her flush against his side, cuddling her as they slept.

He didn't, of course, and the engines roared to life, finally moving the plane down the runway. It wasn't long before they were in the air, and everything around her faded away.

* * *

"Dr. Simco? Dr. Newbury?"

A soft voice penetrated Marie's dreams, and she frowned at the interruption. She and Darren had been on a warm island beach. He was holding her in his strong arms, leaning in to kiss her with those beautiful lips...

"Dr. Simco - Marie! Wake up - we've landed!"

Someone nudged her shoulder, and Marie woke, groaning as she blinked her eyes and tried to remember where she was. She raised her head, confused until she noticed Darren sleeping soundly in the seat next to her. She shifted her gaze to the aisle and saw three amused faces staring back at her. "What - are we there?" She stretched her arms in front of her and then bumped Darren's shoulder to rouse him.

"We've been trying to wake you two for five minutes now," Cynthia teased. "We're in Albuquerque - and the last people left on the plane."

Marie nodded, pushing Darren's shoulder a little

harder this time before she grabbed the back of the chair in front of her and hoisted herself out of the seat. Her hips and knees groaned in protest after being locked in the same position for two hours. She turned to Cynthia, aware of Darren finally moving behind her.

"Which rental company did you book the car with?"

Cynthia pulled a sheet of paper out of her purse and scanned it. "CarServ."

Marie stepped out into the aisle. "Let's go then." She stifled a yawn as she followed her team off the plane.

* * *

"May I help you?" The girl behind the CarServ counter looked as if she was barely old enough to drive.

Marie took the reservation sheet from Cynthia and slid it across the counter. "We have a suburban reserved. The name is Dr. Marie Simco." She smiled pleasantly as the girl took the papers and started entering information into the computer terminal on her side of the counter. "Um..." The girl peered at her over the screen. "I have you down for an extended cab truck. Is there any way you might have reserved that instead?"

Marie looked pointedly at her colleagues and then back to the girl. "There are five of us and a lot of gear, which is why we reserved a suburban. You do have one in, right?"

The girl shrugged. "No ma'am, I'm afraid we don't have any available at the moment. All we have is the extended cab truck. It does seat six," she said, raising her eyebrows. "Unless you'd rather have a sedan..."

Marie rubbed the bridge of her nose and handed over her credit card. "No, we'll take the truck." She wondered how they would all fit into the snug cab, and her skin tingled at the memory of being pressed up against Darren in the plane seats.

Leading the way to the parking lot, she squinted in the bright southwestern sun. It was hot already, and she hoped the truck's air conditioning worked well. They loaded the two hard cases of equipment into the bed along with the luggage, and Nell figured out how to pull the built-in cover over to secure the bed. Cynthia and Nell sandwiched Darren in the back seat, and Marie slid behind the wheel as Scott took the passenger seat. Scott fiddled with the GPS console as they pulled out of the airport parking lot.

"Where are we headed, exactly?" He looked over his shoulder at Cynthia, who shrugged.

"South on Highway 9 until we get to this service road." She held up a map, indicating an utterly deserted part of the state. "The service road leads to an oasis - and the plant should be located somewhere near the water."

He nodded, turning back to Marie. "Are we stopping anywhere before we head into the middle of nowhere?"

"I thought we'd stop in Yellow Rock and get some lunch." She glanced at Cynthia in the rear-view mirror. "How far is the oasis from there?"

Cynthia frowned, examining the map. "I'm not really sure." She was quiet for a moment, and Marie looked in the mirror again to see her frowning at the page. "It seems like it shouldn't be that far though - an hour or so out of town, then ten miles down the gravel road."

Marie nodded. "It's about an hour to Yellow Rock. Is everyone okay until then?"

They all answered affirmatively, and Marie took the next exit onto the highway. She drove in silence, excited to get her first glimpse of the desert. Having been stuck in the lab for several years, she'd forgotten how much she used to love fieldwork. Perhaps when the competition was over and her funding secured, she could plan a few more expeditions.

* * *

Darren sat in the back of the truck cab, his whole body aching from the hotel bed last night, the cramped plane quarters and now the tight backseat where he was in danger of being smothered by the women on either side of him. He'd originally sat on the right side, but the ladies had maneuvered him into the center when they each got in on separate doors.

They had to have planned it, each finding excuses to bump and rub against him constantly. No way was he sitting back here the whole drive into the desert. When they stopped for lunch, he was going to make sure to grab a seat in front, sharing the space with Scott if necessary.

Cynthia's hand was on his thigh again, and he shifted slightly so it would fall away. She turned to the window, and he breathed a sigh of relief when he saw Nell sleeping on his other side. Maybe he'd earned a reprieve.

The hour passed by quickly, and soon Marie pulled into the parking lot of an old-fashioned diner. Darren stretched, grateful for the chance to move around. They ordered and ate in record time. Before he was ready, it was time to get back into the truck.

"Why don't you take shotgun," Scott offered to Darren's surprise. "I'll keep the ladies company for a while." He grinned at Cynthia and Nell, earning a pout from one and a disinterested look from the other.

Darren patted the man on the back before taking his place beside Marie. He stretched his legs under the dash. It occurred to him that Marie was tired too. She'd probably turn him down, but there was no harm in offering.

"Did you want me to drive for a while?"

For a moment, she looked like she was considering taking him up on it. But she shook her head. "That's okay. I can keep going. It shouldn't be too long before we're setting up camp. Thank you for the offer, though." She smiled at him, not quite meeting his eyes. "Later, maybe?"

"Sure." Darren watched her thoughtfully as she pulled back onto the highway, her eyes never wavering from the road. Her profile reminded him of a classic Greek sculpture, high cheekbones and small, perfectly formed nose. Her long, slender neck enticed him, and he turned to look out the window to keep himself from sliding across the seat and grazing his lips over her smooth skin. The small town fell behind quickly, and soon it was just dust and dirt and cactus for miles around.

He leaned his head against the headrest, closing his eyes and letting the hum of the road hypnotize him until suddenly, the engine sputtered and died.

"Crap."

He opened his eyes as Marie coasted the truck off to the shoulder. "What's wrong?"

She took the key out of the ignition, and turned to him with a grimace. "I don't know - it just stopped." She looked back at the dash. "Anyone know anything about cars?"

"Let me take a look," Scott said. Darren looked between the seats, raising his eyebrows. What would a photographer know about cars?

Cynthia opened her door and stepped down, letting Scott scoot out behind her. Marie unbuckled her seat belt and followed them to the front of the truck. Darren hesitated for a moment. He'd been a mechanic for a while in high school to help pay the bills at home, but he was curious to see what Scott could do. He leaned over the driver's seat and pulled the lever that would release the primary hood latch, and then joined the others.

Scott ran his fingers in the crevice just above the grill, pushing the secondary latch down and raising the hood. Once it was up, he started examining the engine, rattling a hose or wire every once in a while. Darren saw the problem immediately, and wondered how long it would take Scott to find it. Someone had obviously sabotaged their ride, but who? Marie wouldn't sabotage her own project, so it had to be one of the other three. Scott either really didn't know what he was doing, or he was putting on a good show to avoid being suspected. Cynthia seemed devoted to Marie and her cause, but people had done worse things than betray their employers. And Nell was still in the back of the truck, apparently uninterested in the whole thing. He wondered if it was because she already knew the problem, or if she just assumed it was normal engine trouble.

"Found it." Scott held up two ends of a wire that should have been connected. "Looks like someone rigged this to rub against that sharp bit of metal there. When it finally cut through, the engine stopped. Anyone have any electrical tape?" Marie and Cynthia shook their heads.

"There might be a toolkit in back, let me look." Darren walked around to the bed and rolled the cover back. He'd seen a small metal box here when they'd been loading up this morning. Maybe that would contain something they could use. He located the box and unfastened the latches. He opened the lid, and let out a low whistle at what he'd found.

Marie came around the other side, barely able to see over the side of the bed. "Did you find it?"

"Not exactly." He carried the box over to her and held the lid open so she could see.

She peered in, her brow furrowing in confusion. "Is that what I think it is?"

He nodded. "I think so – there aren't many things packaged in plastic one-kilo bricks..."

Cynthia and Scott stepped to Marie's side. "That's not electrical tape," Scott said.

Darren closed the lid, carefully latching it down. "This might be the reason the engine was rigged." He stowed the box back where it had been up next to the cab and then climbed down and pulled the cover back over the bed. "One thing's for sure - whoever left those is going to want them back. They were there when we loaded up this morning – I saw the box but didn't look inside. We need to go back to the airport and call the police."

"Even if we could do that, which we can't since it won't start, we've already wasted too much time with delays and problems on this trip. Driving back would take hours, and who knows how long it would take to file a report?" Marie glanced around. "We should be at the oasis by now, setting up and doing a preliminary search for one of those plants." The skin around her eyes crinkled in the bright sun, and she put one hand up to block it. "Can't we just leave the package somewhere obvious, so whoever's looking for it will take it and leave us alone? Or just give it to them when they show up?"

Darren shook his head. "The people looking for that amount of drugs probably aren't using them. They're distributing, which means a lot of money is involved. They're dangerous, and would assume we stole the box."

"They're still human though, right?" She blew out an exasperated breath. "If we just tell them we found it on accident--"

"Newbury's right." Scott stepped forward, placing a hand on her shoulder. Darren wanted to slap it away. "You can't think of drug dealers as reasonable, Marie. They don't listen, and they're probably desperate. We need to go back."

Marie shook her head, narrowing her eyes. "No." Her tone left no room for debate, and when Darren opened his mouth to argue, she held a hand up to silence him. "This is my project, and I'm in charge of this expedition. If you two want to take the truck back, fine - after we find the oasis and get camp set up. We don't have any more time to waste." She turned to Scott. "Can you get the truck running again or not?"

He shrugged. "I still need electrical tape, or something to hold the wires together."

Darren stared at her, noticing the stress lining her face. "I can do it," he said slowly. If she was that determined to keep the truck, they needed to at least get off this main road and move to somewhere less visible. He pulled out his pocketknife and brushed between Marie and her photographer. He might have jostled Scott a little more than necessary.

Ten minutes later, he had the wire spliced together and the truck running again. They all piled in and Marie pulled back onto the highway. Thick tension filled the cab, and everyone was silent as they drove on, watching for the marker to the federal access road.

Chapter Four

"There!" Cynthia leaned forward, extending her arm over the seat and pointing at something off to the right.

Marie jumped, annoyed at the abrupt exclamation. Holding back the snippish remark that came to mind, she looked out the window. A simple wooden sign with plain lettering marked the beginning of Federal Reserve Road Number 9. Marie slowed, carefully turning off the asphalt onto the rough gravel.

Nell spoke up from the back seat. "How far is it to the oasis again?"

Marie was surprised to hear her voice. The tech had been quiet nearly the whole trip, only speaking to order lunch or ask for a bottle of water from the cooler.

"Ten miles," Cynthia answered. She sounded tired, and Marie realized it was nearly dinner time. The gravel road made driving slow, and the sun was sinking low on the horizon.

"There are some power bars and sandwich things in the cooler," she said, glancing in the mirror at Cynthia. "There should be some rolls and napkins in the brown bag back there. If anyone's hungry, help yourself." She heard some rummaging behind her. "Would you mind making me a sandwich too, Cynthia?"

"Sure."

As the light faded, she turned on the dome light for Cynthia as well as the headlights. The desert was coming alive, and she marveled at the small animals that suddenly started appearing off to the side of the road. Little mouse-like creatures darted in and out of their dens, rabbits chased each other and ran at the sound of the engine, and she even saw a coyote watching stoically as they drove by.

Everyone ate sandwiches, and eventually Marie heard rhythmic snoring sounds from the back seat. Checking in the mirror, she noted that all three of them were dozing. Darkness had fallen quickly, and the headlights only illuminated a few feet of road ahead. She glanced at Darren, who had been quiet since they'd found the drugs. Leaning on the door, he had his elbow propped on the edge by the window and his head held up by his fist. He looked at her, and grinned when she looked back.

"Hi there," he said softly. The words were innocent, but something in his voice made the heat rise in her cheeks.

She swallowed, watching the gravel disappear beneath the hood. "You're not sleeping." Mentally, she rolled her eyes. Inane comments were her specialty around attractive men.

"Neither are you," he said, moving closer so she could hear his low quip. "Something I am most grateful for. Do you need a break?"

Marie shook her head. "I'm fine - it shouldn't be long now. I haven't looked forward to crawling into a sleeping bag in a long time though."

"So, do all of your expeditions go this smoothly?"

She shrugged. "I haven't been on one in years," she said, slowing down for a deep pothole. She navigated carefully around it, amazed that the others hadn't woken up with the rough terrain. "As I remember though, it's always something. Not normally drugs. That's a new one."

"Before I found the drugs, I was thinking it had to be sabotage. Scott didn't think the wire was accidentally cut."

The hair on the back of her neck stood up at his words. The thought had occurred to her as well, and she was still uncomfortable with the thought. The only people with access to the truck were in the truck, so if it had been sabotage, it would have to have been one of her team. The thought made her stomach roil.

She tried to keep her voice upbeat. "I guess in a

way it's good that you found drugs in the truck, even though we're probably being chased by dealers now. At least we don't have to be suspicious of each other..."

"Yeah, I guess you're right." She glanced over at him, frowning in the darkness. Something in his tone told her he was still worried. And that worried her.

By the yellow-orange glow of the headlights, she barely saw a large log lying across the road. She hit the brake hard and yanked the wheel to the right in an attempt to avoid a collision, praying that the side of the road was clear.

It wasn't.

The impact was stunning, and sharp pain spread from her shoulder up and down her arm as the seat belt locked. The airbags deployed, and she fought to stay upright, afraid that she'd be smothered in the huge automatic pillow. As the noise and shock faded, she looked around, taking stock of her team.

"Is everyone okay?" She clicked the latch at her hip to free herself and slowly turned to look into the back. Nell, Scott and Cynthia were all staring at her in shock, thankfully held in place by their own safety belts.

"What was that?" Cynthia put a hand on Marie's arm, leaning forward. "Did we hit something?"

"A rock," Darren said. Marie glanced at him, glad to see that he seemed to be okay. She turned back to Cynthia.

"There was a log in the road, I swerved. Into a rock."

To her surprise, Cynthia started giggling. Brows drawn together, Marie looked at Scott. He had cracked a smile too, a hand going to his mouth as his shoulders started to shake. She couldn't help but smile, and wonder what was so funny. She didn't have to ask.

"What's so funny?" Nell shook her head and un-buckled her seatbelt, rubbing the area where she'd been thrown against it. "Dr. Simco here wrecked the truck, and nearly got us killed. And you two are laughing like buffoons." She pulled on the latch of the door, shoving her shoulder against it when it wouldn't open. It still wouldn't budge.

"It is kind of funny when you think about it," Scott said, his laughter subsiding. Cynthia was on the verge of a crying jag. "It doesn't really matter what she did - a log or a rock. Theoretically, we might have actually rolled over if she'd hit the log, so this may have been the better option."

Nell reached over and smacked him on the arm. "It's still not funny. My door won't open. Someone let me out of this thing."

Darren tried his door. "Mine won't open either." He raised an eyebrow at Marie. "What about yours?"

She pulled the latch, and the door swung open. The dome light came on, and she saw why the other doors were stuck. "The truck seems to have slid sideways into the rock," she said, pointing out the far windows. She watched as they all turned to see the rough edge of sand-colored rock pressed tightly to the windows.

She stepped out, and Darren slid across the seat to drop out as well. Cynthia grappled with her door for a moment, clearly shaken. Darren opened the door, and Scott reached over to help unbuckle her seat belt so she could move. She stumbled when her feet hit the ground, and Darren caught her, supporting her while Scott got out, followed by Nell.

"Everyone okay? Any broken bones?" Marie watched as her team shook out limbs and felt their joints, taking stock. One after another shook their heads.

"Just a bruise from the belt," Nell said. She sounded almost sorry that it was the only injury she'd gotten. The others seemed fine, and Darren was fishing around in the truck bed. He found a flashlight, turned it on and handed it to Scott.

"Would you hold this while I check the equipment?" Marie watched as the flashlight illuminated box after box. Everything appeared to be intact, thanks to the bed cover that had miraculously stayed intact. They jumped down, and Scott scanned their surroundings with the light. It appeared to be nothing but empty desert and big boulders all around. Marie checked her watch.

"It's nearly nine," she said, letting out a big breath.

"I guess the only thing we can do is camp out here until morning and then regroup." She started toward the truck. "Anyone want a sleeping bag?"

"Uh, I don't think so." She turned and saw Cynthia and Nell standing together, each with her hands on their hips. Cynthia was shaking her head. "What about snakes and scorpions and creepy crawly desert things?" She walked over to the truck, pulling the back door open. "We're sleeping in the cab, thanks. You guys can take the ground."

Marie shrugged. "You guys want to sleep inside too?" Scott and Darren exchanged a cryptic look.

Scott shrugged. "The front seats lay back...we could all probably fit, if you want to sleep in the middle." They both looked at Marie, and she shivered. She'd slept beside Darren on the flight earlier and ended up with her head on his shoulder. What would happen if she was between these two all night in the truck cab? What if she talked in her sleep? What if she snuggled up to one of them, or worse, drooled on someone?

Marie looked at the ground. There wasn't really a choice. If she refused, they'd know she was uncomfortable, and at least one of them would offer to sleep outside with her. If she said yes, would they get the wrong idea? She took at breath, letting it out slowly.

"Uh, sure, I guess." She started walking toward the truck. "Maybe I'll see if I can sleep in back with the gals. You guys are taller - you could use the extra room." She tried to open the back door, but it was locked. Peering in, she saw that the girls had arranged themselves each with their back against a door, legs stretched out across the length of the seat. She sighed.

"Looks like I'm stuck with you two." She managed to keep her voice from shaking as Darren moved past her and climbed up, scooting over to the far side of the cab. He settled against the door and patted the seat next to him with a grin. Marie met his eyes and suddenly felt as though she was prey crawling toward a predator. She scooted in next to him, the cab getting rapidly smaller as Scott got in and closed the door.

Marie looked straight ahead and slid down in the seat, stretching with one foot under each side of the center console. A warm, masculine thigh pressed gently against each of hers. Thankful for the darkness that hid her blush, she crossed her arms over her chest and laid her head back against the seat. There was no way she'd be able to sleep with Darren so close, much less Scott sharing the same space.

It was going to be a long night.

* * *

The next morning, Marie woke up cuddled next to something deliciously warm. She burrowed closer before she realized that her comfortable pillow was actually moving. Blinking her eyes, a black leather jacket came into focus, and she looked up into Scott's amused eyes.

"Mornin'. Sleep well?"

She pushed off his chest as gently as she could, sitting up on the truck seat. She rubbed her face a few times, trying to get reoriented in the bright morning light. Everything came rushing back, and she turned toward the passenger seat. Darren was staring at her, and while he maintained a calm expression, she felt tension radiating from him as his gaze bored into her. Nervous and uncomfortable, she turned back to Scott, who had shifted toward the door. He climbed out of the truck, holding out a hand to help her down. She knew her cheeks were bright red, and she turned toward the back of the vehicle. There was toilet paper packed back there somewhere.

"Already found it." Cynthia waved the roll at her from her seat on a rock not far away. She nodded and walked over to retrieve it. Walking off into the bushes, she took care of business and then made her way back to the truck. She looked over their supplies, and had a quick conference with the guys while peering under the hood of the truck and then gathered everyone together.

"We need to get to the oasis," she said, shielding her eyes with one hand from the already hot sun. "I think at this point it's closer than going back to the main highway. Darren says the truck should run well enough to get there and then we can send a message back for help with the radio, since there's no cell service out here."

Nell wrinkled her nose, peering around the group to look at the truck. "Uh, I'm sorry, but the truck rammed sideways into a boulder the size of an elephant. How exactly are you going to get it running again, Newbury?"

Darren shrugged. "There's nothing wrong with the body aside from some dents, and the axles are both fine. The engine stopped because the wire I spliced came apart. It's a sturdy vehicle. It will get us there."

Marie smiled wide, hoping her apparent enthusiasm would infect the others. "Okay then," she said, gesturing toward the truck. "Let's go."

She waited until everyone else was belted in and then turned the key in the ignition. The engine sputtered and came to life, earning a round of applause in the cab. She followed Darren's instructions on how to pull away from the rock, and soon they were bumping down the gravel road again. It was much easier to see the potholes and avoid various random objects in the daylight, and she made good time as the sun rose higher.

"Look over there," Scott pointed left. She followed the line with her gaze, her brows drawing together in confusion.

"I don't see anything." Squinting against the sun, all she could see was the yellow sand that covered everything around, and a high cliff in the distance.

"Look closer, at the very edge of that rise over there. See the green?"

He was right. Just to the west side of the cliffs she
saw the first spot of true green they'd seen all morning. "Cynthia, check the map. What kind of land-
marks are we supposed to look for?"

"It just says that there's a valley between two cliffs
off the left side of the road. We'll have to go across
the open desert to get there."

Marie nodded, gripping the steering wheel tighter.
She stayed on the road until they were nearly parallel
with the cliffs and then took a breath and turned the
wheel. The heavy truck sank a little as they entered
the sandy surface, but managed to navigate the rough
terrain well. She went slowly, picking her way through
tufts of cacti and scrub brush to spare the tires.
Everyone was quiet, as if they were holding a collect-
ive breath, scared to let it out lest anything else happen.

"It looked a lot closer from the road," Nell remarked, breaking the silence. "Are you sure we're going the right way?"

Marie wondered why she hadn't noticed her lab
tech's habit of complaining before. Then again, she
expected her team to work, not chat, so she'd never
bothered to get to know Nell. Maybe that was something she needed to work on.

"This is it," Scott broke in. "Look at that, straight
ahead. Trees and shrubs, it looks like."

The side of the cliff looked like it had been taken
over by vegetation. Vines climbed along the rock and

through the trees, some with small white flower clusters growing on the twisted stems. Bushes and trees took up most of the space between the two cliff faces, and Marie parked the truck just to the side near the rock face. The forest was too dense to drive any further.

"I guess we're walking in," she said, turning off the ignition. She checked her watch and turned to look over the seat. "It's about lunchtime. Let's take the cooler out and make sandwiches. Then we'll hike in and look around. We can decide where to set up camp after we get our bearings."

"Great idea." Cynthia opened her door and slid out. "Scott, can you help me with the cooler, please?"

He nodded, and Marie turned around, intending to get out of the truck. She glanced at Darren, his cool stare arresting her movement. Out of the corner of her eye, she saw Nell scoot out. Then she was alone with him.

"Something wrong?" She licked her lips nervously. He held her with his eyes for another minute before he finally blinked.

"I--"

Marie frowned. It wasn't like him to stutter. Was he nervous? Around her?

"I saw you with him in the hall last night."

The words came out in a rush, and she tilted her head, trying to hide her surprise. "You were watching me?"

He nodded. "I just want to know what he's got that I don't. What did you mean by 'men like me'?"

"Um..." Marie looked down at the seat. How could she tell him that he was too good-looking? That just being in his presence caused her mind to stop working and completely idiotic things to come out of her mouth? She shook her head, not even knowing where to start. "You, uh--"

A sharp rap on her window made her whip around, and she was relieved to see Nell outside, sandwich in hand. Marie opened the door.

"You two gonna eat?"

Marie shot Darren what she hoped was an apologetic glance and slid out of the truck. "Thank you," she said, taking the sandwich. She followed the woman to where Cynthia and Scott had set up a little picnic beneath the trees, not daring to look back.

Chapter Five

Darren sat on a low boulder off to the side and finished his sandwich. Marie sat close to Scott, her head bent over something he was showing her. What did she see in him? Darren stood, intending to go over to them, but Cynthia intercepted him.

"How's my favorite lab rat?" She grinned, stopping in front of him and following his gaze to Marie and Scott. "So, think I've got a chance with Scott?"

He frowned. Was she not seeing what he did right now? "I don't know..." He considered leaving it at that, but decided it would be better if she knew. "I think he and the Marie are kind of hitting it off, don't you?"

She looked at him curiously and then surprised him with a giggle. "You really have it bad for her, don't you?"

He shook his head, his cheeks burning. If Cynthia had noticed, who else knew? "Don't be ridiculous.

She'd never go out with a guy like me."

Cynthia tilted her head, giving him a funny look. "Why would you think that?"

He shrugged. *Because she told me so.*

Wrapping her hand around one arm, she hugged it gently. "Honey, any woman would go out with a guy like you. You're hot and smart. Who wouldn't want a piece of that?" Her tone was light and teasing. She grinned up at him, and he couldn't help but smile back.

"I have my flaws." He nodded toward Marie again. "You know her well - what is her type, anyway?"

She reached up to rub the bridge of her nose, squinting at her boss. "You know, I don't know. I've been trying to remember if she's dated anyone since I've known her. I don't think she has." She shrugged, giving him a worried look. "Maybe she goes for girls instead?"

Darren chuckled. "No, she doesn't." He remembered her in his arms, warm, pliant and obviously hot for him. No way was the uptight doctor a lesbian. He looked down at Cynthia, only to find himself the object of a stern gaze.

"You're not guessing." It was a statement, not a question, and he didn't bother to deny it. "What happened?"

"She said she could never be with a guy like me. I've been trying to figure out what it meant ever since. Obviously, Scott isn't like me." He hated the whining tone of his voice.

She laughed. "Not even a little. You two don't act alike, talk alike, or even look alike. Complete opposites, I'd say."

Scott stood up and held his hand out to help Marie up. She brushed off her pants, and they picked up the rest of the containers. As they walked past, Darren could see that she was more relaxed, even smiling a little. Then she caught his eye, and her expression turned serious again. What about him made her so anxious? Was it the kiss they'd shared? Or the good-bye afterward?

He had to know. Today. Somehow, he'd get Marie alone, and make her give him the answers he deserved.

***

Marie felt her face flush as she passed Darren where he stood with Cynthia. She forced herself to nod politely, and kept walking, ice-queen style. It was clear he thought she and Scott had developed a relationship...and they had, but it was purely platonic. She wasn't inclined to set the record straight. Easier to let him think she was interested in someone else than to admit she thought he was too good to be true.

She squared her shoulders. There was work to be done. No use getting caught up in daydreams or dramas.

"Everyone ready?" she called. The others moved

to the truck to strap on packs loaded with supplies and camping gear. She locked up the truck and followed the others as they pushed past bushes into the dense overgrowth. Darren waited for her, and they entered the breach in the cliffs together, the tension between them almost palpable. As she fought her way through the brush, she couldn't help but wonder why she was so drawn to this man? Why couldn't she be attracted to an average guy like Scott?

She looked ahead in time to see Scott disappear over a small rise, Cynthia close behind. Nell must have gone on ahead.

They reached the point where the others had gone out of sight, and Marie stopped short, her breath caught in her throat. The valley laid out below was a stunning mixture of lush green grasses and blooming wildflowers surrounding a sparkling glassy pond that sat slightly off center. It was fed by a low waterfall coming right out of the cliff face, splashing the surrounding yellow rock and revealing beautiful shades of red, orange and brown in the layers. Sunlight filled the valley, spotlighting it for all who happened upon this magical place.

She could get lost here, she thought. She looked down the gentle slope as the others stopped to take some pictures. She'd dreamed of such places her whole life, and now that she was here, she wasn't sure she ever wanted to leave.

A gentle touch on her shoulder jarred her out of

her reverie, and she turned to look at Darren standing next to her. The lines of his face were softened, and in the somewhat shadowed light here at the edge of the valley, with a ray of sun shining sideways across his features, he looked like a Norse god. At that moment, all she could think of was the kiss they'd shared, his body pressed tightly to hers, his arms banded strongly around her. He smiled, caressing the side of her face with one hand.

"It's beautiful, isn't it?" His low voice broke the spell she'd been under, and reluctantly she pulled back. Embarrassed at the fantasy she'd woven around herself, she nodded and looked away.

"It seems like this place could cure many things, not just a simple virus." Mentally shaking herself, she retreated behind her professional demeanor, as she always did. "We should find a place to set up camp. I'm sure it will be much more comfortable to sleep here than spending another night in the truck." She started down the slope, jogging ahead to join the others as they continued to the water's edge.

* * *

Marie collapsed on a log four hours later as she set the last box down in their chosen campsite by the pond. They'd quickly found a flattened area close to the water and protected by the cliffs, and spent the rest of the afternoon hauling tents and equipment from the truck in several trips. Nervous that the drug dealers might see the truck from the service road, she'd moved it around to the far side of the cliffs and then hiked back, a trip that had taken longer than she'd anticipated. Still, it was better than advertising their position.

The others were busy putting up tents, and she pulled herself up to help. They'd already completed the large canvas tent that would house the makeshift lab, and Nell was inside setting up equipment. The large solar-powered generator that had taken three of them to carry sat in a nearby clearing. She hoped it would charge enough tomorrow to power the few machines they would need for testing.

Scott and Darren were setting up a smaller canvas tent that would be the men's quarters, and Marie went to help Cynthia with the women's tent.

"Gorgeous spot, isn't it?" Cynthia fitted two long rods together, creating the main post for the center of the tent. Marie picked up two more, screwing them together and laying them beside a corner of the canvas. These days, most researchers used nylon pop-up tents, but these had been her father's, and they were warm and kept the wind out well. She was loathe to give them up.

"It's beautiful." She glanced around in the dusky light, marveling at how everything changed, depending on the time of day. "If we don't find the cure for the flu virus here, it probably doesn't exist."

Cynthia chuckled. "Look at you - gone from die-hard cynic to poetic believer in just two days. Is it just the valley, or is there a certain someone factoring into your change in outlook?" She winked, and Marie shook her head, the fantasy bubble burst again.

"Just this place, I guess." The words sounded empty even to her, and as she helped raise the canvas onto the poles, she saw a knowing glint in her assistant's eyes.

"He likes you, you know."

Marie frowned, feigning ignorance. "Who?"

It was Cynthia's turn to shake her head, bending over to fasten the ties to thick stakes in the ground. "Don't play dumb. He said you told him you couldn't be with someone like him."

Marie whipped her head around, glaring at Cynthia. She knew her anger was misdirected - it was Darren she was mad at, and rightfully so. Who did he think he was, sharing their secrets with someone else? Trying to keep a grip, she turned back to the tent, securing her side to the stakes.

"What did you tell him?" She congratulated herself on how calm the question came out.

Cynthia shrugged, a grin playing at her lips. "I told him maybe you were a lesbian."

"You did not." Marie walked over to glower at Cynthia, her hands on her hips. "Tell me you did not tell him...that."

Cynthia merely laughed. "I did, but don't worry. He didn't believe me." She leaned in closer. "He told me he knew for a fact that it wasn't true," she whispered.

Marie was mortified. How dare he discuss that kiss...that encounter...with other people? Did everyone know? Were they all laughing at her behind her back now?

She had to talk to him. Or yell at him. Or kiss him until neither of them could breathe.

Turning on her heel, she stalked off towards the men, intent on setting Darren straight on the concept of privacy.

* * *

Darren fastened the last corner of his tent to a stake, straightening to find Marie bearing down on him. She looked ready to kill. He shouldn't have been amused, but couldn't help it. She looked so adorable as she stopped in front of him, her hair falling out of its normally neat chignon in wisps around her face. Her eyes flashed, and when she poked him in the center of his chest, it was like an electric jolt had hit him. Wow.

"Something wrong?" He tucked his hands in his pockets, trying to look casual, but at the same time, keep from reaching out to her.

She opened her mouth and closed it again, apparently needing to compose her tantrum before she delivered it. "Of course something's wrong. You told Cynthia about last night - in my room! You told her everything - how could you? Do you have no sense of privacy at all?"

"I didn't tell her everything. Actually, I didn't tell her anything, she just assumed and I let her. Besides, she's your friend, right? I thought maybe she could help me figure something out." He shrugged, glancing around, wondering where they could go for a little more privacy right now.

"Yes, but that's not something I share with my friends, okay? I don't want people to know things about..." she paused, her rant seeming to run out of steam. "People don't need to know about my personal life. That's why it's called personal. Just don't talk about it anymore, okay?" She stepped to the side, and walked past him, but not before he saw the moisture on her cheeks. He turned and followed her through the trees toward the cliff, letting her get several paces ahead so she wouldn't know he was there.

The moon was rising, and the natural path took them up through a thick grove of trees and into a small grassy clearing. Moonlight spilled across the area, illuminating the green blades as they swayed in a gentle breeze, and Marie's hair as she reached up and pulled the clips out, letting it fall free down her back.

Wow. He'd seen her hair down before at the hotel, but it looked different somehow under the moon. The silky brown strands were highlighted with shimmering red and blonde. He wanted to reach out and run his fingers through it, to feel the softness flowing over his bare skin, as it had last night. She raised her face to the stars, closing her eyes and holding her arms out, as if offering herself to it.

"Why can't you be with someone like me?" The question nearly ripped out of him, he stalked to her, circling her until he could look into her face. She took a deep breath in, letting it out slowly as she lowered her arms. She opened her eyes, fear and uncertainty mirrored in their tawny depths. He reached out to touch her arm, but she stepped back, just barely out of reach.

"It's..." she looked at the ground, wringing her hands. "You're just too..."

"Too what?" He reached out and hooked a finger under her chin, raising her face to his gaze once more. "You can tell me. I can take it. What's so wrong with me that you'd give up this connection between us? Don't bother denying you feel it."

She brushed his hand away. "It's actually not you at all." She turned her back on him. "It's completely stupid, but I can't...I can't be around attractive men."

Darren frowned, sure he'd heard wrong. "That doesn't make any sense."

"I know." She made a nervous sound between a whimper and a giggle. "But I just get totally stupid around men who look like...well...you."

He considered her words for a moment, as a grin slowly spread over his lips. "So...you think I'm attract-ive then?"

"God." She half-turned back to him, as if she wanted to look, but was too embarrassed. "Haven't you been listening? Because I'm not going to say it again. I can't...talk to guys like you. I can't even be around you - I do stupid things like spilling wine and babbling on and on about stupid things no one cares about, making a complete fool of myself and--"

He pulled her to him, her head falling back in surprise. He leaned down and covered her mouth with his, praying she wouldn't pull away. When she wrapped her arms around his neck and pressed against him, he smiled against her mouth.

"You don't need to talk," he whispered onto her lips. "You don't need to do anything. Just let go, follow my lead."

Chapter Six

Marie let herself melt into him as he whispered against her lips. She kept her eyes tightly closed. Maybe if she didn't look at him she wouldn't screw this up. She reached up, her arms shaking as she locked her fingers behind his neck. He wrapped his arms around her waist and pulled her tight to his body. Opening for him, a shiver of anticipation traveled through her neck as his tongue stroked inside her mouth, coaxing hers to come out and play. She couldn't remember anyone ever kissing her with such passion. He held her firmly, as if he thought she might bolt at any minute.

He pulled back, and she whimpered in protest. He chuckled, and she waited for his lips to find her skin again. But they didn't, and she grew nervous, scared that her fears were being realized. He didn't want her after all. She lowered her head, opening her eyes to stare at his chest. She couldn't bear to look at his face, to see the rejection she knew must be in his eyes.

"Look at me." His voice was rough, and she pushed against his chest with her hands, wanting to put some distance between them. But he held on tight, trapping her in his arms. "Marie, sweetheart, just look at me."

Sweetheart? She stopped struggling and took a deep breath, holding it in as she raised her gaze to meet his eyes. His expression was serious, his touch gentle, and he rewarded her bravery with a quick kiss and then pulled back.

"I want you."

His words were simple, flattering, but Marie couldn't help but frown at the statement. Why would he want her? She had average looks, her glasses were geeky, her hair was a mess and she couldn't even manage to keep her cool around him, always screwing something up or worse, blushing at everything he said. Why would anyone want her?

"Why?"

He was the one who broke eye contact then, looking at the ground as if he were seriously considering her question. Even he didn't know why he wanted to be with her, apparently. She pushed at his chest again, and he turned his gaze back to her.

"Because underneath all your fears and shyness, you are an extremely intelligent woman who wants to help people, and I find that incredibly sexy. You don't realize how beautiful you are, and every time I'm near you, I want to grab you and kiss you senseless." He leaned down and kissed her again, gently nipping her bottom lip before he started kissing his way down her neck. He pushed her collar aside, placing gentle kisses across the top of her shoulder, and then drew a slow line with his tongue back over her collarbone to the base of her throat.

Marie shivered, not from the cold, but from his hands sliding up under her shirt, caressing her ribs as he coaxed the fabric higher. His fingers were warm, his touch light but insistent as he pulled it over her head and stepped back, just looking at her. The cool night air wafted over her almost bare torso and she shivered again, with only her plain white cotton bra covering her puckered nipples. She hugged her arms over her breasts, self-conscious and wishing he'd just hold her again.

He knelt down, tugged her forward and wrapped his arms around her waist. "God you're beautiful," he said, his breath hot on her stomach. He kissed her belly button and pulled her down in the grass, reaching behind her to deftly unhook the clasp of her bra with one hand. When he started to slide the straps down her arms, she reached up and stopped him, holding his hands with hers.

"You first," she said, her voice shaking. If she was going to bare all for him, the least he could do was reciprocate.

He grinned, sending a jolt of pure arousal through her body. "Okay. I'll play fair." He leaned back slightly and reached over his head, pulling his polo off in one smooth stroke. Marie stared at the broad expanse of his chest, tanned and glowing in the moonlight. It was obvious he worked out - he didn't have an ounce of extra fat on his body. She tentatively traced the hard lines of sculpted muscle. She'd always dated average looking men - never one who looked like a work of art.

He flinched when her fingertips made contact, and she jerked her hand back, looking up with an apology at her lips. But there was no judgment, only tenderness in his eyes, and he took her hand, placing it over his heart.

"It's okay. I want you to touch me." His voice was soft, soothing as she returned to her exploration. Braver, she smoothed both hands up and down his chest and lower, over his rib cage and down to dip a finger shyly into his waistband.

He groaned, and clasped her to him, dispensing quickly with her bra and lowering his head to take one of her hard nipples in his mouth. She jumped at the sensation, arching her back instinctively. He placed one hand behind her back, his other caressing her hip. She moaned, the waves of desire coursing through her as he unbuttoned her jeans and eased the zipper down, moving his mouth to her other breast. His tongue swirled around the sensitive tip and she whimpered, lacing her fingers through his hair and trapping his mouth against her.

He slid a hand inside her jeans, and she rocked against him as he inched his fingers between her legs. Overwhelming sensations coursed through her, shaking her to her core. His fingers rubbed and swirled at her clit as he placed kisses down the center of her chest. She was trembling, weak, and she wondered how she'd ever survive such an intense assault on her senses.

His strong thigh slid between her legs as he propped himself up on his elbows above her. He stroked her hair away her face, staring into her eyes.

"Are you sure..."

She understood, and appreciated his thoughtfulness as she nodded, smiling up at him. She wanted him inside of her. Now. "Yes." He bent down to kiss her again, this time different, more possessive, and she felt herself letting go, her mind foggy with passion.

Suddenly a scream pierced the night, followed by a frenzy of shouting.

* * *

Marie let out a long breath as Darren rolled to the side and stood. He pulled her to her feet with an apologetic look.

"Come on," he said, passing her shirt to her. She nodded, her brain still trying to switch into thinking mode. "Stay behind me."

"Okay." She followed him out of the clearing, sprinting toward the camp as another scream rang through the valley. It wasn't far, and upon arrival, she immediately saw the reason for all the noise. She stared in disbelief at her colleagues as they ran toward the water, away from the campfire. Beside the fire pit, illuminated by the flames stood a small black creature with a tall, fluffy tail. On its back, a signature white stripe gleamed brightly, and eau de skunk wafted on the breeze. Darren grinned back at her.

"Guess it's a good thing we weren't here." He winked and then walked toward the pond, careful not to approach the skunk as it waddled toward the far edge of the camp. Marie followed, her heart still pounding, though she wasn't sure if it was from making out with her lab tech, fearing for her team, or the promise in Darren's gaze.

"About time you two showed up." Scott waded back up onto the shore, his eyes scanning the bank before he stepped out of the water. "Did you see our little visitor over there?" Marie wrinkled her nose. He had definitely not gotten out of the way in time. She took a small step back.

Darren nodded. "It wandered off, I think. The screaming might have scared it a little."

"Did anyone else get sprayed?" Marie peered around him, squinting as she tried to see Cynthia and Nell in the water through the darkness. She could hear them splashing just a few feet off the shore.

Scott chuckled. "Poor Cynthia got most of it, and I think I got the rest. Nell was the smart one - she ran straight for the water." He turned, cupping his hands around the sides of his mouth. "You can come out now, ladies." He started walking toward the fire with Darren, and Marie followed. She tried to remember what compounds would remove the smell aside from tomato juice, which they didn't have.

"I'll be right back," Marie said, veering toward the lab tent as Cynthia and Nell joined the men at the fire. The smell pervaded the camp, and she hoped they had enough supplies to make what she needed.

She flipped on the flashlight that hung just inside the tent flap, and unhooked it from the strap, using it to locate the supply boxes in the far corner. Rummaging through them, she found hydrogen peroxide, baking soda and liquid soap. She emptied a bucket and carried the supplies to the others.

Cynthia looked up from her seat on a log, frowning. "Where have you been?"

"Solving your problem," Marie said, careful to keep her voice calm. "You and Scott are going to have to strip down, and wash with a solution I'll mix up. Go get some clean clothes, and I'll have it ready when you get back." She watched Cynthia trudge toward her tent and turned back to the others.

Scott had already taken off his jacket and shirt, and Marie noted his wiry muscles, unable to stop herself from comparing them to Darren's. Scott had more of a swimmer's physique, long and lean. Darren's body was more sturdy and compact like a wrestler. One side of her mouth curved up just a little as she remembered that she didn't care much for fish.

Cynthia came back, clean clothes in hand, and Marie picked up the bucket of supplies. "Scott, I'll mix some solution up for you after Cynthia's done - it's not stable, so you'll need to use it right away. We'll be right back."

Scott walked off toward the men's tent, and Marie led Cynthia down to the bank and away from the fire. Thirty minutes later, the stench in the camp had subsided to a more bearable level.

* * *

"I think those two should room together," Nell said, poking at the fire with a long stick. "They both still have a skunky smell. They could take the men's tent, and Newbury can bunk with us for a night or two."

Darren glanced across the fire at Marie. She looked wilted, but raised her eyes to meet his at Nell's words. He wasn't sure what he expected to see, but it wasn't the spark of panic that lurked in the pretty green depths. He frowned. After what they'd shared in the clearing, he had thought that they had an understanding of sorts. He'd hoped that she'd finally accepted him, accepted their shared attraction, and would be receptive to exploring it further.

But as she lowered her gaze again, he felt like she was shutting him out. Was she having second thoughts? Was it really his looks that made her uncomfortable, or was there something she hadn't told him? Maybe something that didn't have anything to do with him. He needed more time with her. More time to show her she could trust him.

"I think that's a good idea," he said, looking over at Scott. "Do you mind rooming with Cynthia for a night or two? Sorry, but you do still sort of smell." He softened the statement with a grin, and Scott shrugged, glancing over at Cynthia.

"Ladies' choice," Scott said, watching her carefully. Darren glanced at Cynthia. He couldn't tell with only the light from the fire, but she seemed to have a little more color in her cheeks. He wondered if there was something going on between the two.

" I…uh…guess that would be okay," she said. She looked over at Marie, who shrugged. Darren guessed she was worn out, both physically and emotionally.

He stood, stretching his arms over his head. "I suppose we should turn in then. I'll just get a few things out of the other tent."

"I'll come with you." Scott followed him over to the tent, switching on a flashlight once they were inside. "So where were you guys?"

Darren held back a grin. "We were just checking out a clearing behind the camp," he said, reaching for his duffel and gathering up his sleeping bag from where he'd already spread it out on a cot. "Thought we'd get an early start scouting for that plant." He tossed the sleeping bag over one shoulder and turned. The expression on Scott's face said he didn't believe the story.

"Yeah. Right." The photographer smirked, his arms folded over his chest as he blocked Darren's path. "That's why she came back without her bra, right?"

Darren shrugged. Damn. He'd have to go back and get the bra before someone else found it. "Do you have some sort of claim on her? Because it looked like you had your eye on someone else just now by the fire..."

"I just don't want to see her get hurt." Scott stepped aside so Darren could exit the tent. "Be careful, Newbury. Anyone can see she's not like other women."

Darren considered that as he walked to the other tent. No, Marie wasn't like other women. She was shy and naïve and easily spooked. She was also incredibly hot and attracted to him. He could work with that. He reached the women's tent and caught himself before he barged in.

"I'm here," he called out. "Everyone decent?"

"Just a sec."

A few murmured whispers ensued, with some rustling before the tent flap finally pushed open, and

Cynthia stepped out followed by Marie. They both merely glanced at him before heading off toward the other side of camp. He shrugged and went inside.

"That one's yours." Nell stood at the back of the tent, pointing to a cot near the entrance. "I hope you don't snore - I'm a very light sleeper. And keep your pants on - I don't want to see whatever it is you've got."

Darren nodded, stifling a chuckle. "Yes ma'am," he said. He put his gear on the ground and spread his sleeping bag on the cot, keenly aware of her watching his every move. Everything settled, he turned, inclining his head respectfully toward her. "I need to take a quick walk. I'll knock or something before I come back in."

"Thank you," she said, finally turning away.

Relieved, he left, taking quick strides across the camp to the trail he'd followed Marie up earlier. He'd retrieve her bra and leave it with her things. With any luck, she would be sleeping by the time he got back.

* * *

Marie swung the flashlight side to side over the tall grass, frantically searching for her bra. It was bad enough that Scott had noticed the lack. She'd seen his eyes go straight to her chest when he first came out of the water, and he'd actually had the gall to wink at her. She'd been cold, and her nipples had been poking at the thin material of her t-shirt. Why couldn't women control that, anyway?

She'd told Nell and Cynthia where she was going - there was no use hiding it, since they'd both noticed too. Cynthia had wanted details, and Nell had warned her that there would be no hanky-panky in the tent that night. Marie had assured her it had been a big mistake; one she wouldn't make again.

She spied something white fluttering near a rock, and walked over to check it out. It was just a wild daisy, bobbing in the night air. She ran one hand through her hair, letting out a deep breath as she looked around the clearing again.

A twig snapped behind her, and she turned, her heart racing. How much adrenaline could one person take in a night? Rather than a bear or other equally scary creature though, she came face to face with Darren, her bra dangling from one of his fingers.

"Looking for this?" He moved his hand, sending the article swinging from side to side, the stark white material nearly glowing in the moonlight.

She nodded, wading through the grass to snatch it from his hand. Just as it would have slipped off, he closed his fingers, trapping it in his grasp.

"Give it to me." She realized her mistake when his eyes blazed with heat at her words. He grabbed her wrist, pulling her in for a heart-stopping kiss.

Even as her body melted against his, Marie allowed herself only a moment to enjoy the feel of his warm lips on hers. Then she put her hands against his chest and pushed, hard enough to break free of his magnetic pull. When he stepped forward, reaching for her again, she took two more steps back, holding a hand out to stop him.

"No," she said. She took a moment, waiting for the fog of arousal to clear so she could think. "No. We can't do this. Not here. Not now." She dropped her eyes from his cold, disbelieving stare to focus on his chest instead. "They all know what we were doing out here, and it's already causing a distraction. This project means too much...it's everything to me. We can't waste time on...on this kind of thing."

He folded his arms over his chest. "That's not why you're putting distance between us." He paused, and she slowly raised her eyes to his face. He head was tilted slightly, and there was no anger in his tired eyes as she'd expected. Only disappointment. "You're scared. You want me. You want what we could have together, but you're scared that it's not going to work out, that something will go wrong and you'll get hurt." He looked up to the sky, and her breath caught in her throat at his beautiful, strong profile in the moonlight. It was as if she were staring at a sculpture, chiseled in stone. An unattainable icon.

"Maybe." She looked down at the ground for a moment, considering. She looked up, resolute. "It doesn't matter. I won't be pursuing this with you, and I expect you to respect my wishes. Our relationship will stay on a professional level from now on, Dr.

Newbury." She stepped around him, and made her way down the path, not looking back to see whether he followed her or not. She didn't care. She was tired, and as she made her way through the camp to their tent, she wished that when she woke up in the morning, she'd find herself back in her cozy little apartment, rid of this very bad dream.

Chapter Seven

The next morning as Marie woke from a coma-like sleep, she felt someone watching her. She kept her eyes closed, breathing in the sweet, musky scent that had already been burned into her brain as Darren's. If she waited long enough, would he leave? She didn't want to rehash last night's conversation or listen to his pleas to try again. Why couldn't he just leave her alone?

"I know you're awake."

His voice invaded her thoughts, and she wasn't sure if he'd spoken or if she'd merely dreamed it. She took a deep breath, and let it out in a long, slow sigh. Then she opened her eyes, and Darren's face came into focus just inches from her own. He smiled.

"Good morning." He reached out with one hand as if to stroke her face, but stopped short of touching her, pulling his hand back to rest on his knee. His expression turned serious. "I just wanted you to know. I'll respect your wishes while we're here, working on this project."

She nodded, giving him a tentative smile. "Thank you. I appreciate that, Dr. Newbury."

He looked away for a moment and then back at her. This time the heat was there, and she drew away a little from the intensity. "After this is over though, you and I are going to explore this attraction between us. You deserve it. We deserve it. Never doubt that I want you." He stood and turned, walking out of the tent without looking back.

She blinked, trying to remember how to breathe. She must still be dreaming. No man was that perfect. Men like him didn't pine for women like her. They certainly didn't lust after average-looking scientists who were more comfortable with diseases than people. She closed her eyes again and then opened them before unzipping her sleeping bag and swinging her legs over the side of the cot. Rubbing her face with her hands, she sighed and got to her feet to gather her things. Dream or no dream, it was time to get moving.

* * *

Fifteen minutes later, she strolled into the lab tent to find Nell and Cynthia already at work. Nell tipped her head toward a makeshift table in the corner.

"Coffee and trail mix over there for breakfast."

She turned back to the trays of test tubes she was setting up, preparing for the samples they planned to collect today.

Marie went over and poured herself a cup of coffee. She took a tiny sip, not bothering to ask who made it. She never drank coffee out of the lab pot, preferring to brew her own at work. Out here, there was no way around the group pot though, and she was relieved to find that it wasn't the sludgy brew that Nell often made.

She wandered over to another table where Cynthia was preparing another set of test modules. "Where are the guys?" she asked, trying to keep her tone casual.

"Scott said he wanted to take some pictures without us telling him what to shoot," she said, a smile playing at her lips. "Darren is checking on the generator. There wasn't much sun yesterday, and he's worried there won't be enough power to run the cooler."

Marie nodded, checking her watch. "Can we be ready to go in an hour?" She put her coffee down and opened the box that contained the centrifuge, laying the pieces out on the table in order.

"I think so," Nell said. Cynthia nodded, and Marie set about assembling the machine in front of her.

"So..." Cynthia looked over at Marie, a mischievous look in her eye. "Did you get your bra back?" She winked, and Marie felt the heat rising in her cheeks.

"Yes." She pointedly looked back at her machine, trying to discourage further questions.

Cynthia walked over to stand beside her. "Well? What's going on with you and Darren? You two seemed to hit it off..."

"It was a mistake." Marie glanced up at her friend. "A relationship with a team member would be distracting and could slow our work down. We can't afford that." She kept her eyes on the parts in her hands, not wanting to see the disapproval on her assistant's face.

"That is possibly the saddest thing I've ever heard."

Out of the corner of her eye, Marie watched as Cynthia walked away. She looked back at the table, trying to focus. But the statement bothered her. Why was it sad to be practical, to think of the team and put her career first? The chances of a lasting relationship with Darren were much less than the chance of winning this competition and securing funding for her work. Weren't they?

A sharp pain jolted her out of her thoughts, and she realized she'd cut herself on a metal edge while trying to fit two wrong parts together. She looked around, spying the first aid kit by the tent's entrance. She bandaged her finger and then checked her watch. Time to find some plants.

* * *

Darren pushed past a low tree branch, hot, sweaty, and longing for a cold beer. He'd waded through dense vegetation for three hours, but hadn't seen anything remotely like the description they'd been given by the locals back at the diner in Hopi. They'd tried to pay someone from the town to guide them, but there was a superstition that in order to use the powerful medicine in the plant, one had to discover it for themselves. He wasn't sure how that would work as far as Marie's idea to take the plant back with them and cultivate it in a lab for medicinal uses, since it probably meant there was something about the plant's environment that prevented it from growing anywhere else. But if anyone could figure it out, it was Marie's team.

Everyone had agreed to meet at the camp around noon, and he turned back in the direction the camp lay, taking a different route than the one he'd started on. He went slowly, examining the tree branches closely for any sign of the small specimen. The leaves should be spear-shaped, with darker dots on top and red veins on the bottom. The light pink flowers were tiny, and it was said they glowed in the moonlight. The whole plant was no larger than a baseball, and it was reported to have an affinity for growing in the crook of a tree branch.

He'd just moved to a new area when a shout rang out somewhere to the north. He marked the tree he'd been looking at with a piece of twine, and then ran toward the sound. He passed through a copse of trees and into a clearing. Another shout guided him to the east and back into the forest.

The others were already there, and barely glanced up at him as he joined them. They were all looking up into the branches of a tall, thick tree, necks strained with the effort as they moved around trying to get a better view.

"Is it up there?" He stepped back, craning his neck as the others had. Marie gave him a curt nod, looking as if she were about to speak.

Cynthia turned with a wide grin. "It's right there, where that second lowest branch meets the trunk." She turned back, pointing in the general direction. "Can you see it?"

He looked where she was pointing, squinting in an effort to make out anything that looked like a small plant with pink flowers. He shook his head in defeat. "I don't see it."

Scott motioned him over to where he was standing. He held the camera so Darren could see the screen on the back. "Better?"

He nodded. The plant appeared on the screen just as it had been described. It looked healthy and even appeared to be blooming.

He glanced over at Marie as she bent over her pack rummaging for something. "Need something?"

"We have to go back to the camp and get some rope, maybe some packing material. I was just looking for something more colorful to mark the tree with."

He thought about it. "Maybe someone should stay here," he suggested. "It's easy to get turned around out here, and it would be a shame to lose the location, since the plant is so elusive."

"You're probably right." She stood up, addressing the group. "I need someone to stay here while the rest of us go back to camp and get rope and bigger collection pot so we can take the whole plant. Any volunteers?"

"I will." Scott spoke up before Darren could respond. Cynthia tentatively raised her hand, casting a shy glance in Scott's direction.

Marie nodded, appearing not to notice. "Okay, you two can stay. We'll bring you some lunch. Do you have enough water?" They each held up a plastic bottle with clear liquid nearly to the top.

"Okay then, let's get going so we can collect the plant before dark." She led the way through the trees toward the camp, and Darren followed Nell, glancing over his shoulder as he walked away. Scott had taken a seat at the base of the tree, and Cynthia was lowering herself to the ground beside him. He couldn't help but feel a tinge of jealousy, not over Cynthia, but rather over the relationship the two seemed to be forming.

* * *

An hour later, Marie led the way to the tree they'd found earlier, getting turned around once or twice, but eventually finding her way. She was grateful Darren hadn't said anything about her misguided sense of direction. She had a feeling he'd known every time she made a wrong turn.

She was acutely aware of his presence, and it made her crabby and anxious. His promise that they would explore their attraction further after the project didn't help. Cynthia's words rang in her head, over and over, getting her defenses up all over again. Silently, she went over all the reasons that Darren was a bad idea, her thoughts swirling around and around. Cynthia was practically sitting on Scott's lap, her lips locked to his and his hand on her breast.

Marie froze, not quite sure what to do. Nell kept walking past her, and shook her head.

"Get a room, you two. But do it later. We've got to get that plant out of that tree - if someone didn't steal it while you were making out like monkeys."

Just over Marie's shoulder, Darren chuckled. "Looks like they didn't get bored," he murmured into her ear. He brushed past her, his arm rubbing against hers and sending tingles of electricity through her skin. Not fair.

Scott and Cynthia had risen, and were brushing themselves off. Deciding to ignore the incident, Marie took the rope from Darren and held it up.

"Who has the best throwing arm?"

Everyone was silent, looking around at everyone else. She shrugged, looking up at the branch they needed to reach. "Anyone want to try climbing it? I have some hooks in my bag..." She paused, not really surprised when Darren stepped forward.

"I'll do it." He crossed to her, and she nodded, diverting her gaze to paw through the bag for the grips.

Holding them out, she found herself anticipating contact just before he took them out of her hands. How was she supposed to keep her cool when the most innocent touch had her wanting more?

"These...uh..." She took a breath and tried again. "They're...you use them like rock climbing grips. Screw them into the...trunk, then use them as supports while you reach up with...uh...the next one." She could feel the heat in her face, knew the others could see her blush. What was wrong with her? Darren nodded and turned toward the tree.

"Scott will you spot me?"

Marie was grateful when everyone moved toward the tree as Darren screwed the first hook in just above his head. She bent down to get the rope. He could take it up with him and pull her up. Then she could collect the plant. She wanted to be the one to do it, so she could record every detail of how it grew on the tree. They'd need to recreate the environment to cultivate the plants in the lab later.

She stood, rope in hand, and took a step toward the tree before stopping short. Damn. He'd taken his shirt off, and now she was faced with the sight of his tanned muscular back, rippling as he reached up and tested the grip with his weight. He turned around, and caught her staring. A grin spread over his lips.

"Is that for me?" His voice was low and deep, and she was completely mesmerized at his spectacular body in the daylight.

"Dr. Simco." Nell's irritated voice broke through her brief trance. "Stop drooling and give the man the rope. Good lord, what's gotten into you people?"

Marie lowered her eyes, humiliated. She, of all people, should be able to act like a professional. Her reaction to this man was just embarrassing. She handed Darren the rope, steeling herself against the desire. Not daring to meet his eyes, she strode back to her bag, taking out her water bottle as if nothing had happened.

"Here goes."

She tilted the water into her mouth before glancing back over her shoulder. Everyone watched Darren as Scott boosted him up to the first grip and then supported him as he screwed in the next. With the rope over his bare shoulder, he looked like a very hot explorer on his way to make a fantastic discovery. She capped the bottle, shaking her head at the irony. It was all true, actually - they were exploring, and they had made a discovery that could revolutionize treatment of viruses all over the world. Little had she known that they'd have an actual icon on the trip.

Finally feeling slightly less humiliated and reason-
ably certain her face wasn't bright red anymore, she
rejoined the group, shading her eyes with one hand as
she watched him climb. As those tanned muscles
rippled smoothly higher into the branches, she found
herself wondering why she was resisting his advances
so hard. What were the odds that such a gorgeous
specimen would ever want her again? He got to the
branch and carefully straddled it, and then took the
rope off his shoulder and unrolled it, feeding it down
to Scott. He tossed the other end over the branch
above him and caught the end, creating a fulcrum to
pull with.

"Are you ready to come up?"

His voice wafted gently down from above, and she
nodded, not sure how she would focus while being up
there with him. She stepped forward and took the
rope from Scott, deftly tying it into a makeshift sling
that she sat in. She grabbed the first grip and looked
up.

"Ready," she called, thankful that her voice was
steady. The rope went taut, and she used the grips to
support her weight as he pulled her up.

"That is one fine lookin' man," she heard Nell say
from below. She grinned. At least she wasn't the only
one affected by Darren's body. Suddenly feeling light-
er, she didn't hesitate when Darren reached out to
pull her the rest of the way up. She took his hand,
feeling secure in his strong grip as he helped her to a

position in front of him on the branch.

"Welcome aboard." His breath was warm against her neck, and she fought the urge to lean back against him. She slid forward until she was close enough to examine the plant and the way it attached to the tree.

The roots actually grew right into the tree. Old leaves and detritus had accumulated where the branch met the trunk, and from that angle it wasn't hard to ascertain that water washed nutrients from the decaying bits right over the roots of the plant.

"Like a bromeliad," she murmured, so focused on the little eco-system in front of her that she didn't feel Darren moving up until he was touching her back, his thick thighs bracketing her own.

He leaned forward, looking over her shoulder, and she couldn't help but feel his groin pressed against her buttocks. Was that his arousal she was feeling? Trying to ignore it, she went back to work, prodding gently at the surprisingly thick roots on the tiny plant.

"I hope you don't mind," he said, his face just inches from hers. "I want to watch."

Chapter Eight

It was all Marie could do not to melt against him as the words caressed her ear. She wobbled a little on her perch, biting back a gasp as strong fingers wrapped around her rib cage, steadying her.

"Careful," he said, amusement in his words. "I didn't mean to throw you off guard."

Sure he didn't. She took a breath, let it out slowly and sat up to unhook the collection bag from her belt. The movement put her in direct contact with his chest, and he chuckled. Rolling her eyes and mentally coaching herself to focus, she extracted the piece of burlap she'd stowed earlier and scooped some of the decaying leaves into the center. Laying it carefully in front of her, she leaned forward and started the delicate task of prying the plant roots off the tree, breaking off bits of bark wherever the roots wouldn't let go. When all the edges were loosened, she leaned farther forward, carefully using a pocketknife to cut out the soft wood under the center of the plant. When it was finally free, she wrapped it in the burlap and poured water from her canteen over the pouch before placing it back in her bag.

Taking a breath, she put the knife in her pocket, and wiped her brow with the back of her forearm. She leaned back to stretch her stiffening muscles, and suddenly remembered she wasn't alone. Strong hands supported her waist mid-stretch, and held her in place when she tried to lean forward again.

"Relax," Darren said, squeezing her ribs lightly. "Nice job. Ready to get out of this tree?"

"Ye--" A sharp crack rang out, and the wood shifted underneath them. She grabbed Darren's legs, fear and adrenaline speeding through her body. "What was that?"

" Put your leg over the branch." He nudged her right leg, and she shifted so both her legs were on the same side. "I'm going to grab the rope – swing over to the trunk nice and easy. Do it now."

She pushed off the branch, and a series of vibrations sent her plunging into open air as the wood fell from beneath her. She dropped a few feet and then stopped short when the rope caught, jerking her sling to a halt.

"Darren!" She twisted, relieved to see him hanging from the other end of the rope, though his muscles were corded with the effort. "How do we get down?"

She looked at the ground, noting the rest of her team had gotten out of the way. Darren's side of the rope didn't quite reach the ground, and his position was a little lower than hers.

She dropped a few inches, and gasped, looking instinctively toward Darren. Her eyes widened when she saw him slowly feeding the rope over the branch through his hands, his whole body straining with the exertion. "What are you doing?"

"I'm," he paused, his breaths coming in shallow bursts, "going to lower you down. Scott should be able to reach you when I run out of rope."

The rope slid a couple more inches, and she fought to hold herself upright at the jerky motion. "What about you? Without my weight you'll fall!"

He paused, taking a deep breath and letting it out. "You'll eventually pull me up to the branch. I'll climb down to the grips after you're on the ground." He continued letting the rope out, and she watched him rise inch by inch. She looked down. Scott was standing below, waiting.

Marie reminded herself to breathe as the ground got closer. She looked up, relieved to see that and Darren sat on the higher branch now, making sure her descent was slow and controlled. Finally low enough for Scott to grab her waist, she was standing on solid ground a few seconds later.

"Oh thank god." Cynthia ran up to pull her into a hug. "Are you okay?"

Marie awkwardly patted her shoulders before pulling away. "I'm okay."

She looked up. Darren had moved to the center of the tree, and was carefully navigating his way through the steep angles back to the grips. It took a few seconds for him to maneuver his foot onto the first one, but after that, he made good time coming down the trunk.

It was all Marie could do not to run to him as soon as his feet touched the ground. She felt a strong urge to wrap her arms around him and make sure he really was okay, with nothing out of place. She held back though, staring awkwardly as Cynthia ran to him and pulled him into an embrace.

"I'm so glad you made it," Cynthia cried, hugging him tightly. He hugged her back, his eyes never leaving Marie's. When Cynthia released him, he held out the grips to her and walked toward Marie. "Wait - your hands!" Cynthia grabbed his wrist, stopping him to examine his palms. "You need to clean those out and bandage them so they don't get infected."

Nell stepped up to take a look. "Yep - that's some bad rope burn there. We'd better get back to camp - I have some ointment we can bandage them with." She walked over to Marie and grabbed her hands, glancing at the abraded skin. "You too. Let's go." She headed for the trail. Scott raised his eyebrows and followed.

Cynthia pulled Darren along until they reached Marie. He gently slid his arm out of her grasp with a

smile. "You go on - we'll be right behind you." She
nodded, flashing them both a knowing grin before
she turned away. Marie looked up at Darren, tilting
her head to the side.

"Um...so thanks for not letting me fall." She
lowered her gaze, suddenly fascinated with the beads
of sweat accenting the muscles in his chest. He
stepped forward, pulling her to him, and she went
willingly, closing her eyes and reveling in the feel of
his body against hers. He was sweaty and smelly, but
she didn't care. He could have been hurt or killed in
that tree, and he was the only reason she'd made it
down alive.

"Hey," he said softly, pulling back enough to look
down at her. He slid a finger under her chin, lifting
her face. "You're welcome." He leaned down and
pressed his lips against hers in a feather-soft kiss that
made her want to sigh. It was over too soon, and he
smiled at her and stepped away. He took one of her
hands, ignoring the biting pain in his own, and pulled
her toward the forest with him. She followed willingly, not sure she could deny him anything he asked
at that moment.

***

The forest was a cacophony of crickets and bugs
as the sun sank slowly, and Darren was glad to see the
tents as they crested a small hill half an hour later.
He'd had to let go of Marie's hand some time ago,

when the adrenaline wore off and the pain set in. Now he was just tired and wanted nothing more than a hot shower, a good meal and a soft bed. He'd settle for a wash in the pond, a dried meal pack and his sleeping bag.

He glanced back over his shoulder, concerned when he saw the exhaustion on Marie's face as she followed him over the uneven ground. He waited for her to catch up, returning her weak smile with one of his own. She seemed to be softening toward him, and he wished they were anywhere but in a desert oasis, racing the clock.

"We're almost there," she said, nodding toward the tents. " I might just be hallucinating a bathtub on the horizon." She brushed past him and he followed, down the low rise and around the pond's bank to their temporary home.

Scott stepped to the rock pit, stacking some wood in the center. "I'll get a fire going if you want to wash up."

Darren nodded gratefully at Scott and grabbed a change of clothes and a towel. He wandered down the banks past a large pile of brush where he'd be shielded and stripped down, flinching as he waded into the cold water. It sluiced easily over his skin, instantly cooling and soothing his weary muscles. He used the t-shirt he'd discarded at the tree as a wash rag, rubbing off the sweat and grime with as much vigor as he could muster.

Finally starting to feel human again, he waded toward the bank, the night air making him shiver as it wafted over his wet body. Then he stopped, his instincts kicking to high alert. Someone was watching him from the bank. He continued, slower, until he was just ankle deep in the water. He could just make out the slender silhouette on the beach. Had Marie finally come to him?

"Mind if I join you?"

Disappointment rose in his throat as he stood there, covering himself with his shirt as Nell approached. She had undressed as well, and he averted his eyes as he slid on his shoes.

"I just finished," he said, walking over to the rock he'd left his clothes on. He quickly pulled on his sweats and then turned to her, gathering the rest of his things. "I was just headed back to get some food, so it's all yours."

"You're wasting your time on her, you know. She's a cold bitch - you'll never get into her pants."

Darren turned at the cruel words and stalked over to her. "You don't know anything about it," he said, his fingers curling into fists. "Why do you work with her if you don't like her?"

Nell shrugged, her hands on her hips, making no attempt to cover herself. "She's the best - or at least that's what they all think. I work with her, and if get a good reference, I'll be able to run my own team someday." She stepped closer, running a finger down the center of his chest. "I'm just using her...like I want to use you." She gave him a wry smile. "Or your body, anyway." In a quick movement, she reached up and wound her arms around his neck, pulling his lips down to press against hers with more strength than he'd given her credit for. He pushed her away, the force nearly sending her sprawling.

"Don't ever try that again," he growled, turning away. "Just stay away from me."

He walked back along the bank to the camp, where Scott and Cynthia were sitting by the fire.

"Where's Marie?"

Scott frowned. "I thought she was with you - she went off in that direction." He pointed in the direction Darren had just come from. "Didn't you see her?"

It was Darren's turn to frown. "No...I just saw Nell, but..." He had the sudden urge to hit something as the answer occurred to him. "Damn." He dropped his things and ran back the way he'd come, scanning as well as he could in the darkness for her. Had she seen Nell kiss him? He had to know, had to make sure she understood.

* * *

Marie stood behind the thick brush, not believing the scene before her. She'd been going to the pond to rinse off, hoping to run into Darren. She wasn't sure what she wanted from him, but he made her feel things - want things - she hadn't wanted in a long time. And after today, she just wanted to feel alive, maybe even take a risk, and see what happened after that.

She'd gotten there in time to see Darren walk toward a very naked Nell, who pulled his head down for a passionate kiss. Her eyes filled with moisture and she turned away, ducking into the wooded area as the sound of footsteps drew near. She couldn't bear to face anyone - the hurt and embarrassment were too much. Making her way through the woods to the camp, she slipped into her tent. Not bothering with the flashlight, she undressed and donned her thermal underwear, ignoring her sticky skin as she crawled into her sleeping bag. She zipped herself in, and closed her eyes, willing the image of Nell and Darren out of her head.

It felt like only minutes later that she woke to someone rustling in the tent. She opened her eyes a little, peering through her lashes in the dark, expecting to see Nell by her cot. Instead she saw a decidedly male figure bending over her, the expression on his face unreadable in the dark. She quickly closed her eyes again, hoping he hadn't notice her peering out.

"I know you're awake," he whispered. "We need to talk."

She opened her eyes again. "No, we don't." She kept her voice low in case Nell was already in bed.

"Just let me sleep."

"Sorry - can't do that."

He slipped one hand below her shoulders, the other below her knees, and scooped her up. She couldn't hold back a small shriek of surprise as he carried her out of the tent, sleeping bag and all.

"Put me down!" She struggled to get her arms free, but she was wrapped up so tightly she could barely move. "I'll go with you, just put me down."

He grinned down at her, and just kept walking. "Nope. I kind of like carrying you like this. Makes me feel tough, caveman-style. Stop wiggling or I'll drop you."

She stopped struggling, realizing that the slippery material could slip out of his grasp at any time. "Where are we going?"

"Did you get to rinse off earlier? I didn't see you at the pond."

Marie barely held back a snort. No, he hadn't seen her, but she'd seen him. "I decided to go straight to bed. I was tired." He stopped, lowering her gently down to the ground. She finally got her arms free and sat up to glance around, dismayed that he'd brought her to nearly the exact spot where she'd seen him kissing Nell.

"Strip down."

It wasn't a request, she noted, and she pulled the sleeping bag back up over her arms, hugging it around her shoulders. "No." Did he seriously think she was going to be seconds for him tonight? One naked body was more than someone like him deserved.

He stood up, pulled his shirt over his head and unbuttoned his pants. She watched, mesmerized as he pushed them off, standing naked and aroused in the moonlight. He moved toward her, and she shrank back. She wanted him, there was no denying that. But there was no way she could give in, not knowing he might be sleeping with someone else.

"You can either strip, or I'll do it for you." He took another step closer, the corners of his lips lifting slightly. "I'll admit, I prefer the latter." He reached out and pulled the two halves of the bag, forcing the zipper to slide down its length.

She scrambled to her feet, just out of his reach. "Turn around," she said, giving in. He gave her a nod, and turned his back. She pulled off her thermal top and pants, hugging her arms over her chest as she shivered in the cool night air. "This is crazy - it's too cold." She took a couple steps toward the water and turned back. No way was she getting in that water right now. She'd freeze.

She bent over to pick up her clothes and suddenly she was in his arms again, being carried swiftly into the pond. Water splashed up and hit her bare skin as he waded out, sending chills over her skin until she was finally enveloped in the freezing liquid. "Oh. My. God." She clung to him, her arms around his neck and her body pressed tightly against his to capture what little warmth she could.

"Just relax," he murmured, his hands scrubbing over her body in vigorous strokes. "It will only take a few minutes."

Her teeth were chattering. "I--I'm n-n-not going to l-l-last a f-f-few m-m-minutes." A big shiver traveled in waves over her body, and she knew she would never be warm again.

He took her arms, lowering them from his neck, and she hugged them against her chest as he scrubbed the rest of her down. Then he gathered her up and strode back to the shore, stopping long enough to pick up their clothes and her sleeping bag before he carried her further into the forest. Dropping the bag on a grassy patch under the trees, he lay down, pulling her across his torso. He wrapped them both in the down-filled material and held her close, her head pillowed on his chest.

"You saw me earlier, didn't you?" His deep voice rumbled in her ear alongside his heartbeat. "With Nell."

She nodded, not trusting her voice. She fought the urge to push away, still too cold to give up the body heat. She steeled herself against the excuses she knew were coming.

"She came on to me, Marie. I told her I wasn't interested and left."

She pushed at his chest, frustrated when he tightened his arms around her and held her in place.

"You went back. You kissed her," she said, her voice cracking. She tried to stifle the tears that threatened her tenuous composure.

"Because she insulted you." He rubbed her back, the motion soothing. "I went back to defend you, and she kissed me. I pushed her away and then went looking for you." He ran a hand over her hair, lifting his head to press his lips lightly on hers. "I wanted to see you, to make sure you were okay."

Marie shifted a little, moving her legs to a more comfortable position. One that brought the evidence of his arousal to her attention as it nudged her inner thigh. "So you decided to abduct me - and my bed - to dunk me in cold water?" Only half-serious, she kept her tone light and tried to focus on the moment rather than anything that had happened before or the regret she'd surely feel tomorrow. The heartbeat under her ear sped up, and she grinned, shifting over him again.

"Careful," he warned, his voice raspy. "Don't do something you might regret."

Marie propped herself up on his chest, lifting her head so she could look into his eyes. "I'll regret it, definitely. But tonight I'm not going to think about regrets." She stroked a shaky finger down the side of his neck and trailed it down his throat. "Tonight I'm thinking about pleasure." She leaned down and pressed a tentative kiss against his throat, blocking out the little voice in her head that told her to stop before it was too late. "Pleasure you've been promising me for too long now. Time to pay up."

* * *

Her touch was electric, pulsing through his body to awaken every nerve under his skin. He was ready for her almost immediately, had been ready ever since that kiss in the hotel room, and he couldn't believe it was finally going to happen. He threaded his fingers through her hair, gently coaxed her head down, and then pulled her in for a soft, slow kiss.

He ran his tongue gently across her lips silently asking for entry, and plunging deep when she acquiesced. His tongue swirled over and around hers as he ran his hands down her back to dip into the hollow at the base of her spine. He caressed the firm swells below, squeezing and pulling her up his body. Dampness slicked over the tip of his cock, and he moaned against her mouth as he realized how wet she was for him.

She nipped his lower lip once and slid lower, impaling herself on him in one firm thrust. She took all of him, and he could feel her stretching to accommodate his size. The feeling nearly drove him mad as he held her still, afraid if he moved it would be over too quickly.

She lifted her head to look at him, her eyes glittering in the moonlight as she pulled up, nearly unsheathing him and then plunged back down hard. She set a steady rhythm, riding him harder, faster until he was at the edge, just waiting for that last push to send him over.

He reached up and rolled her nipples lightly between his fingers. She swirled her hips sending hot pulses throughout his body. She tightened around him with a cry, throwing her head back as she reached her climax, and he thrust hard one more time, following her into oblivion. Her name slipped past his lips as she collapsed over his chest, and he held her there with no words to describe what had just happened between them.

Slowly the world came back into focus, and he felt her heartbeat slowing. He skimmed his fingers over her back, up and down, enjoying the sensation of her smooth skin under his fingertips. Pressing a kiss on her temple, he noted her lips curled up in a satisfied smile. Had he ever seen that expression on her face before? He didn't think so, and it pleased him to think that he'd put it there. She shifted, pushing the flap of the sleeping bag back a little and letting the cool night air seep into the warm cocoon they'd created.

"Everything okay?" He wanted to bite his tongue for letting the question slip out when met with pointed silence. He'd hoped this would be a turning point for them, a new start. It was starting to feel more like a one night stand. Marie got to her feet and rummaged through the pile of clothes at her side.

"Uh, yeah. Sure." She pulled her shirt over her head and shimmied into her long underwear before tossing his shirt and sweats to him. "We should get back. The others will be wondering where we are." She stepped into her shoes and stood over him, her arms crossed over her chest. Waiting.

He sat up and pulled on his shirt, frowning up at her. "What's wrong, Marie? Did I hurt you, or..." He stood, pulling on his pants.

"No." She gave a nervous laugh low in her throat, the sound making his cock twitch again. "God no. I'm fine. Better than fine, really. It's just..."

He stepped toward her, reaching out to her, but she stepped out of reach. "Just what? Talk to me."

She took a deep breath, staring over his shoulder in the direction of the pond. "It's just too much," she said finally, looking at the ground. "I've never...it's just scary. I need to think."

It was his turn to chuckle. He pulled her into his arms, rocking her side to side in his embrace. "No thinking," he teased, pulling back enough to smile down at her. "Just let it be what it is." He bent his head and kissed her, relieved when her lips moved under his. Forcing himself to step back, he caressed the side of her face with his hand one more time. He slipped on his shoes and then tossed the sleeping bag over his shoulder and reached for her hand. She laced her fingers with his as they walked back through the trees toward the camp.

Chapter Nine

Marie's senses were on hyper-alert as she walked in the moonlight beside Darren. Every sound, every scent seemed intense. Even the air on her skin invoked a prickling sensation that she could only attribute to what she'd just experienced. He was the embodiment of every one of her fantasies, and she felt both elated and scared to death at how powerful her feelings had become for him already.

He wouldn't stay. He would tire of her eventually and find some gorgeous, confident, sensual creature that could rock his world, and she'd be left alone again. She looked up at him, wistful The question wasn't whether they had a future - she knew they didn't. But did she dare take advantage of his interest while she had it? Was she strong enough to take what he wanted to give and then watch him walk away?

They reached the camp, and she realized it wasn't

as late as she'd thought. Scott and Cynthia sat by the fire, backs propped against a log, and heads bent together in quiet discussion. Nell must have gone to bed. Marie extricated her fingers from Darren's warm grasp, immediately feeling the loss.

"I'm going to find something to eat," she said, keeping her voice low. "Want anything?"

He nodded. "You go ahead, see what you can find. I'll put this in the tent, and be right behind you." He grinned and placed a quick kiss on her lips before he turned away with her sleeping bag. She watched him for a few seconds and then headed to the lab tent to see if there were any sandwich supplies left.

* * *

A loud shout woke Marie the next morning. Her eyes shot open, and she scrambled off the cot as angry voices penetrated the tent walls. Hurrying into her clothes, she rushed out, running to the lab tent where the chaos seemed to be centered.

"What's going on?" she asked as she entered the lab. She quickly scanned the interior, stepping over to the table where everyone had congregated.

Cynthia held up the bag in which Marie had stored the plant, frustration lining her face. "The specimen is missing!" She looked down at the empty square of burlap, holding only bits of bark and leaf mold now. "I was going to start preparing samples for testing, and it's gone!"

Marie frowned. "Could it have fallen out? Has anyone else seen it since we got back?" She looked around the room, bending over to peer underneath the tables. Nell's voice broke into her cursory search.

"We looked everywhere, Dr. Simco. Turned the place inside out. It's just not here."

Marie merely nodded, not daring to look at her tech. She still couldn't get the image of the woman naked out of her head.

She turned her attention to the table, examining the surface closely. "Could an animal have come in and stolen it? Was the bag open or closed?"

"It was just like you left it," Cynthia said, pointing to a spot off to the side. "Right there, all wrapped up and in the bag. Someone went to the trouble of removing the plant and putting everything back exactly like it was." She looked around, her eyes holding on each person's face for a moment before moving on. "There's no one else here. It had to be one of us."

"Let's not start throwing accusations around." Scott stepped over to her, rubbing her neck with one hand. He looked at Marie. "Is there any way to know for sure we're the only ones here?"

She shrugged. "According to the locals, there's only the one way into the valley - the way we came. It's a big oval surrounded by cliffs. Anyone else would have had to come down the same way we did."

"So it's possible we have company." He fell silent.

Nell frowned. "What about whoever left the drugs

in the truck? Think they could have found us down here?"

Marie rubbed her forehead with one hand. "If it was them, why take a plant? Why not just take their drugs and leave?" She glanced over at the far corner, where the white metal box was stashed out of the way.

"She's right - and they probably would have woken us all up, at least." Darren stepped closer to her, his nearness comforting. "It had to be someone who knows how important that specimen was."

"Which means it had to be one of us." Cynthia looked over Marie's shoulder, to where Darren was standing. "Someone who used to work for our competition, perhaps?"

He stepped out from behind her, and Marie glanced up to see his jaw tighten. "Are you accusing me of working for Adams?" He took another step towards his accuser, and Scott moved to block his path. "You think I would do something like that to Marie?"

"It makes sense." Cynthia tilted her head, considering. "Adams wants to win - the easiest way to make sure Dr. Simco loses her funding would be to pay someone to sabotage our last chance. Who better than a hunky technician to seduce Marie and sabotage her project? Sounds like you get paid twice - or was the seduction thing a freebie?"

Marie gasped, her eyes widening. It all made perfect sense. She fought to keep her composure, humiliated at how easily she'd given in to him. She'd wanted to believe he wanted her, but maybe she'd been right all along.

"Is it true?" She held up a hand when he started to speak. She wasn't sure she wanted to hear the answer. "Don't bother. It's the only thing that makes sense. Aside from Scott, you're the only person who wasn't a member of my team before."

"At least hear what he has to say before you go and hang the man, Dr. Simco." Nell shook her head, frustration lining her face. There's no need to jump to conclusions here. It still could have been any one of us."

"He worked for Adams," Marie said, blinking back tears. "You and Cynthia have been with me a long time. Are you saying you'd throw it all away for the right amount of money, Nell?" She paused, glancing at Scott. "Cynthia hired you, and convinced me to hire Darren too. Heck, maybe you're all in on it. Maybe I can't trust any of you."

"Marie, listen to me." Darren took a step toward her. "I'd never--"

She shook her head. "I don't know who to believe right now. I don't even know if my friends are who I thought they were." She looked at Cynthia and dropped her gaze to the table. This is why she didn't get close to people. In the end, the only person she could trust was herself. The wise course of action would be to just keep working, and hope to figure out who was responsible before anything worse happened.

"Get your gear," she said, her tone firm. "We're going out to find another sample." She avoided looking at Darren as she took the burlap off the table and folded it back into her bag. She walked to the entrance of the tent, turning to find them all staring at her. "What?"

"What about him?" Cynthia pointed to Darren, his eyes glittering with anger.

Marie shrugged. "He comes with. No one stays at the camp alone from now on."

"And if I refuse?" His voice was low, and she worked hard not to step back at his menacing tone. She didn't want to believe it was him. Didn't, really. But there was no way to know if she could trust him. Or anyone.

"In that case someone will stay here with you. I don't care who. Hell, you can all stay if you want. I'll get the plant myself." She turned and pushed out of the heavy canvas flaps into the morning sunshine. It was all a bluff, and she was sure the others knew that. There was no way she'd be able to get a sample out of a tree, let alone do all the testing and recording necessary by herself. She trudged to the pond, bending over to fill her canteen with water. She never should have listened to Cynthia. She should have just left the university and started over somewhere else.

"I deserve a chance to defend myself," Darren

said, squatting down to fill his own water bottle. "You owe me that much."

"I don't owe you anything." She avoided looking at him, staring off into the trees instead. "I just...why did you sleep with me?"

"I like you. I'm attracted to you. I didn't sabotage your project, Marie. I'd never do anything to hurt you. All I ever wanted is--"

She held up a hand. "Stop. Just stop." She took a breath, doubt mingled with anger. What if he was telling the truth? She exhaled slowly. She wanted to trust him, but how could she know for sure? "I--I can't do this right now. I have to focus, and do whatever I can to protect my career."

"And your heart?"

The gravel crunched behind them and she turned, relieved to see the rest of the team approaching. She waited for them to get water and then led them into the trees, going in the direction of the place they'd found the plant yesterday. With any luck, they'd be able to procure another sample before long, and get back to the camp in time to prepare samples for testing tomorrow.

* * *

Several hours later, Marie stopped under a huge old tree similar to the one they'd found yesterday, its branches gnarled and covered with twisting vines. She peered up the trunk, and Darren stood back from the group, observing. Scott and Nell were high on his suspect list. Scott was the only outsider to the profession, and the most likely to take money for sabotaging Marie's project. Nell was abrasive, but that didn't necessarily point to someone who'd betray her boss. The fact that she'd come on to him made him wonder if she hadn't been trying to make waves between him and Marie though, which put her on his short list of suspects.

Cynthia could have done it, but he wasn't sure what her motive would be. In all the time he'd known her, she'd seemed genuinely dedicated to her boss and their work. He glanced over at her as she spoke quietly with Scott as they examined another nearby tree. It hurt that she'd helped him get this job and then accused him of sabotage. Did she really think that little of him, after all this time?

"There! There's one right up there." Marie's triumphant voice rang out, bringing the others running. She pointed up into the ancient tree, and he moved closer for a better vantage point. He knew any offer of help would be rebuffed, so he remained quiet.

Scott moved up to stand by Marie. "Want me to climb up first?"

"No..." she paused, studying the slightly inclined trunk. "I'll climb up myself." She turned to Nell. "Hand me the rope, please."

Nell slid the coil off her shoulder, handing it off to Marie. She opened her bag and pulled out the grips, handing those over as well. Marie went over to the tree, set the first grip and then hesitated before finally handing the rope to Darren. "Can you toss one end over that branch? I'll use it as a secure line."

He took the rope and swung out a long length in a wide circle, finally tossing it neatly over the branch. He passed the remainder to Marie, her fingers brushing his and sending a quick shock through his skin. She looked up, her gaze holding his for a brief moment before she turned to secure the rope around her waist. He moved to the other side of the branch, wrapping the shorter end around his own waist and tying it off tightly.

"Maybe I should do that..." Scott stepped forward, but Darren waved him off. Marie was giving him a chance, trusting him with her life. He'd keep her safe.

She got the sample bag, put the strap over her head and neck and braced her toes on the first grip before pulling herself up. She stretched to put a second grip in and then moved up, repeating the process until she reached the elbow that housed the plant specimen.

Darren watched as she braced herself on the last grip, staying against the tree trunk rather than going out on the branch as they had last time. She leaned out, laying the burlap in front of her and going through the same process to detach the plant as she had the day before. Darren watched her face as she worked, fascinated at all the different emotions that flickered across it. Her brow was furrowed with concentration, her lower lip caught neatly between her teeth as she worked on a particularly difficult spot.

It took about half an hour to free the plant, and he noted a slight tremor in her hands as she tucked the burlap package back into her bag. He tightened his grip on the rope and took in some of the slack, hoping she had enough grip strength left to descend.

"I'm coming down," she called, glancing his way. He nodded, and she started backing down the trunk, her progress slow as she removed the grips behind her. Darren played the slack out little by little as she moved, glad when her feet finally touched the ground again. He watched as she tried to untie the knot at her waist with trembling hands.

Making short work of his own, he went to her, lightly brushing her hands away. "Here, let me," he murmured, deftly releasing the rope and freeing her.

"Thanks." She glanced up at him, her beautiful eyes so sad and tired he wanted to pull her into his arms and carry her back to camp. Knowing she wouldn't welcome his touch, he nodded and stepped back, focusing on coiling the rope as the others gathered their things.

"Are we going back to camp then?" Cynthia waited beside Scott, a hopeful note in her voice.

Marie nodded. "Yes...no, wait." She paused for a moment and then looked at Nell. "Why don't you and Scott keep looking for another specimen. If you find one, bring it back to camp. Cynthia and I will start preparing samples for testing, but we should have a second plant on hand, just in case."

Cynthia held up a hand. "Could I go look for more plants instead? Nell can prepare the samples just as well..." Her voice trailed off as Marie shook her head.

"No." She glanced at Scott and then looked back at Cynthia. "I'm not blind. I know you and Scott have a...a thing going on. I think you two will work better if you work separately." She started walking back toward camp, and Darren watched as Cynthia looked longingly at Scott before following her boss.

* * *

When they reached the lab tent, Marie took the burlap package out of her bag , setting the sample on a clear area of one table. She used a sharp knife to cut off one leaf and half of a long root and set the rest of the plant aside.

"Cynthia, you can prepare the leaves. Darren, start on the roots. I want preliminary results by tomorrow morning - we only have a few more days to find something and get everything back to the lab. I'll take care of the plant and then get the equipment ready."

Cynthia glanced at Darren, eyebrows drawn together. "You're going to let him work on this? After what he did?"

"We still don't know that it was him," Marie replied. "Why are you so sure, anyway? It was your idea to hire him."

"I just thought since he worked for Dr. Adams..."

Marie held up a hand. "If you thought he'd be a risk and he is working for Adams, then it's on your head too. So think carefully about where you're going with this."

She avoided looking at Darren and turned back to the table. "There's nothing I can do for now and there's more work than I can handle alone. So if you want to help, get to work." She bent down, and pulled a coir pot out of a box on the ground. She heard movement behind her and took a quick peek over her shoulder, relieved to see both of the techs had moved to empty spots at the table to work. Thank goodness. She wasn't sure what she'd do if either of them had balked. All that mattered right now was the work.

Chapter Ten

Five hours later, Marie stood, arching with her arms overhead to stretch her sore back. Sleeping on a cot all night and then hunching over a low table all day was rough on the body. She looked around, noting the fatigued lines on her team's faces. Nell and Scott had come back an hour before with two more specimens, and Nell ran some early tests while Scott photographed the plants, various parts and molecular structures through the microscopes.

"Let's break for dinner, gang." Marie went to the food storage box and took out a stack of military-style meals, handing one to each team member. They all filed out of the tent toward the fire Scott had started again. Marie sat on the ground and leaned back against a large log across from Scott and Cynthia. Nell chose a spot to the right, and Darren to her left. Underneath the smell of sweat and grime, his personal musky scent prevailed, and God help her, she wanted him. *Damn pheromones.*

She studied her team as they ate. Could she trust any of them anymore? She'd have to replace her entire team when they got back at this rate. She thought about all the people her drugs could benefit, and sighed. It was worth the trouble. So few people focused on natural cures due to the expense and difficulty. She felt a responsibility to keep pressing forward.

"Dr. Simco – should we take shifts guarding the plants? We could rotate every few hours, so there's always someone watching the tent."

Marie looked up when Cynthia spoke. There was something odd about the woman's tone. Was it a good idea to assign guards, when she wasn't sure who she could trust? She considered her options and then shook her head.

"I don't' think so." She glanced around at the surprised faces of her team. "I'm going to move my things to the lab tent. I'll sleep in there from now on. That way I'll know if anyone goes in or out." She looked over at Cynthia. "You need to move back in with Nell, and Darren will sleep in Scott's tent."

"Is that really necessary?" Cynthia looked over at Scott and then back to Marie, anger in her eyes. "I've worked with you for a long time now, and I resent that you'd think I had anything to do with this."

Darren shifted beside her, and Marie tried to ignore her body's immediate response. "She doesn't trust anyone right now." His calm tone belied the frustration in his eyes, and she wished she could reassure him. All of them, for that matter. It was still hard to believe anyone in the group would want her to fail, and somewhere deep down she still hoped it wasn't true. But caution seemed to be her best defense at the moment.

She sighed, the stress of the day taking it's toll. "I'm the only person here who has everything to lose if this expedition fails. All of you might have something to gain from my failure. So I'll guard the research and the plants. Then the only person to blame if something goes wrong is me."

Nell stood, brushing her jeans off with her hands. "Fine by me. If you don't mind, I'm going to get a few more things done and then turn in."

"Wait, I'll go with you. No one works in the lab alone from now on." Marie stood too, and felt rather than saw Darren getting to his feet behind her. She glanced back at Cynthia, who just stared at the fire. "I'd suggest you get your things moved now, both of you." She looked at Darren. He didn't seem all that bothered by her new rules. He winked, and she turned away, feeling the heat rise in her face. She followed Nell to the lab, hoping the rest of the evening would pass quickly.

* * *

Darren gathered Marie's things first, carrying them to the lab tent. He set them up just inside the flap, although she was too busy to notice. Bent over a microscope, a few strands of her hair escaped the band she'd pulled it back with. He watched for a moment as she adjusted the knobs and made a notation before switching slides. Her movements were efficient, and he tried to reconcile the scientist before him with the sensual creature he'd pleasured just the night before.

Movement caught his attention from the corner of his eye, and turned to see Nell frowning at him. He shrugged and exited the tent, nearly running over Cynthia as she wrestled with her duffel and sleeping bag.

"Let me help you with that." He reached for the sleeping bag that she dragged behind her.

She pulled away, glaring at him in the near darkness. "No. I can get it." She walked towards the women's tent, weaving over the uneven ground until she finally pushed through the entrance. Darren snapped the flashlight on, illuminating the interior.

"I'll get my stuff out of your way," he said, bending down to gather up his things. She dropped hers in a pile, collapsing dramatically onto Nell's cot to wait. He stood, staring into her eyes for a long moment. "Why do you think I'd sabotage Marie's work? You know how long I've waited to work with her - why would you think I'd throw that all away?"

Fear flashed in her eyes for just a moment before

it was replaced with anger. "You're the only logical choice," she murmured, glancing away. "You worked with Dr. Adams before - why wouldn't you still be loyal to him?"

"You don't really believe that, do you?" He tilted his head, frowning. "There's something else - something you're not telling me." He stepped closer, looking down at her as she stared at the ground. "What are you hiding?"

"Nothing! Leave me alone! Help!"

Darren stepped back as heavy footsteps sounded outside. "That was low," he said, holding the tent flap open for whoever was coming to her rescue. Scott, he'd bet. "I'll find out what you're hiding - count on it."

Scott hurried into the tent, going straight to Cynthia and kneeling down beside her. "What – what's wrong? Are you hurt?"

"N--n--no." She turned a pathetic look on him, her lower lip just barely sticking out in a pout. Darren wanted to roll his eyes at her little show. "It was just a misunderstanding. I'm fine."

Scott turned, narrowing his eyes. "What did you do to her?"

Darren held up both hands, taking another step back. "Nothing, man. Relax. Everything's cool. Right Cynthia?"

She nodded, looking toward the front of the tent as Marie and Nell both parted the front. "We're fine.

I'm sorry."

"So everything's okay?" Marie looked from Scott to Darren, a confused look on her face. He bent down and collected his stuff.

"Just moving my things," he said, tilting his head to her on the way out. "Nell, would you accompany me to the lab, please? Don't want people to think I'm messing around in there by myself." Nell looked at Marie and then stepped outside, waiting for him to follow.

He followed her across the camp, and she held the flap open as he took his things inside and dropped them beside Marie's. Nell watched, her hands on her hips as he laid out his sleeping bag under one of the tables.

"You know she's not going to let you sleep in here," she said, pulling up one of the folding canvas chairs to sit in. "I think you're probably the last person she wants to be around right now."

"I know." He finished arranging his things next to the tent wall, and went to one of the tables, running his hand over a rack of slides. "She doesn't get a choice though. I'm not letting her stay here by herself when there's a potentially dangerous person in our midst."

"I thought it was generally agreed that you're pretty high on the list of 'potentially dangerous people'. Though for what it's worth, you don't seem like the type to me, even though you did work for the competition."

He shrugged. "Working for Dr. Adams was just a means to an end – the end being working with Marie. I'll do whatever I can to make sure she's safe. I'm not leaving her alone."

"Suit yourself." She pushed out of the chair, reaching for a pair of gloves. "I may as well get some work done while I'm babysitting you." She handed him a stack of papers. "Here. See if you can find anything in these preliminary results that might be useful."

He took them and sat in a vacant chair, switching on a flashlight to save the generator power for the equipment. He started reading, scanning through lines of analysis as Nell worked. If he could just find something, anything, it would prove that his motives were innocent.

* * *

Marie entered the lab tent to find Nell working at the back table and Darren reading documents in a chair. She frowned when she saw his things piled under one of the tables, his sleeping bag laid out neatly beside them.

"Why aren't your things in your tent?"

He looked up, disoriented as he stared at her. "I...uh..." He held up the papers. "You need to see this. I think I found something."

She walked over to stand at his shoulder, noting

that Nell had turned and was listening too. "What is it?"

He pointed to a section near the bottom. "Look at those numbers - does that indicate what I think it does?" He handed her the sheet, and she picked up the flashlight, shining it directly on the paper.

"It may be - Nell, did you do these tests?"

Nell peered at the results, nodding. "Yes - Dr. Newbury was doing the analysis for me. Could that be the combination we're looking for?"

"Maybe. It sure looks good." Marie handed her the paper, trying to contain her excitement. She'd learned long ago not to put her hopes in unverified results, but if this compound was the right one... "Let's run with it. Run this sample through a complete battery, and take careful notes. Have Scott photograph everything as you do it. I want this ready for an extensive workup once we get back to the university."

"Will do, boss." Nell set the paper down on the back table with the slide attached and then laid a box on top of it to ensure it wouldn't go anywhere. "I'll get on it in the morning. Now that you're here to keep an eye on that one," she nodded her head at Darren, "I think I'll get some sleep."

Marie smiled. "Thanks Nell. I appreciate it." She waited until the tech had gone and then turned back to Darren. "So, I'll ask again - why are your things here?"

"You shouldn't be sleeping here alone. It's not

safe."

She crossed her arms over her chest, leaning on the edge of a table. "And you think you're the best person to keep me safe? Or you just want to be here when I fall asleep so you don't have to sneak in later?"

"If we're both here and something disappears, you'll know it was me, right? If someone else comes in, you'll have backup. This way you can keep an eye on me, and I can watch out for you. We both get what we want." He leaned back, propping one arm over the back of his chair. She wasn't sure if she should slap him, order him to get out, or kiss him senseless.

She maintained eye contact for a long moment, finally giving in. "Fine." She straightened and then walked over to where her stuff was still in a pile. "You can stay. But if anything goes missing tonight, you're responsible." She spread her sleeping bag in front of the entrance. Anyone coming or going would have to step over her. There was no doubt it would wake her up. She'd always been a light sleeper.

She glanced over at Darren, surprised to see him shimmying out of his jeans. "What are you doing?" She dropped her gaze to his sleeping bag, not wanting to be reminded of the lean, muscular legs she'd been shamelessly draped across last night.

"Getting ready for bed." He sounded amused. She shook her head, sliding into her own makeshift bed, grateful for the mattress pad she'd hauled over earlier. It had seemed like too much work to bring the whole cot.

She turned onto her side, facing him and saw that he was fully encased in his sleeping bag, one bare arm curled over the top edge. She clicked off the bright lantern next to her, plunging the tent into darkness. She listened to him get comfortable, and wondered what it would be like if they were somewhere else, somewhere work and money didn't matter.. She closed her eyes, imagining that they were alone here in this paradise, cuddled up together in a cozy lover's tryst. She drifted off, smiling as she dreamed.

* * *

Chirping birds and a light breeze blowing under the canvas woke Marie the next morning. She lay still for a few moments, just enjoying the fresh air and sounds of nature. As her brain woke up, she remembered where she was and why, turning her head to glance around the tent. Nothing looked out of place from her vantage point, but she was on the ground. She unzipped her bag and rolled out, shivering at the brisk morning air.

"Sleep well?"

Startled, she turned to see Darren sitting on his sleeping bag fully clothed, eyebrows raised in question. "Um, yes," she replied. "Thank you. And you?"

He shrugged, one corner of his mouth tipping up

in a mischievous grin. "As well as I could, sleeping alone and all." He crawled off his bed, folding it in half before he stood. "Anything missing?"

Steadying herself with her hands, she pushed to her feet. She went to the nearest table and checked over the contents. "Doesn't look like it," she said, moving to the next and then finally the third. The specimens were still there, and the slides and research that Nell had been working on all seemed to be accounted for. "I think we're good," she announced, walking back to her sleeping bag and pulling it away from the entrance. Putting her things neatly in a corner, she pulled her hair up in a ponytail and pushed up her sleeves.

"Good morning." Cynthia walked in, looking entirely too happy. Marie stifled the urge to roll her eyes. It was obvious someone had spent the night in the wrong tent again. "Everything here?" Cynthia walked over to the coffee pot.

Marie nodded. "I think we're ready to start working. If Nell's preliminary tests pan out, we can head home tomorrow."

"Ahead of schedule - I like it. I'll just get the coffee going, and run those tests." She shot Darren a big grin on her way out.

He smiled at Marie and shrugged. "Someone got lucky last night. I wonder how Scott's doing this morning."

"Feel free to go find out." Marie turned her back

on him, snapping on a pair of latex gloves. "Everyone else can do what they want - I'm going to work."

Chapter Eleven

Darren didn't want to leave her here, upset and working alone. He watched, wishing there was some way he could make things right, but the set of her shoulders hinted that she was closed to any advances. The smell of coffee wafted into the tent. Apparently Cynthia had decided to just make it by the fire this morning, and he couldn't resist one cup. Maybe a little caffeine would help her mood as well.

"I'll get a quick cup of coffee - want me to bring you one?" He waited for a long moment and then turned to go. She probably hadn't even heard him. A murmur from her direction caught his ear before he got out of the tent.

"Sure, whatever."

He grinned. There was hope after all. He left the tent and strode down to the fire where Cynthia and Scott were sitting together. "Can I steal a couple cups of that?" He pointed to the coffee pot, glancing around the immediate area. "Where's Nell?"

Scott shrugged, looking around. "Haven't seen her."

"Me either." Cynthia looked toward what had been the women's tent. "Maybe she's still sleeping."

Darren poured coffee for himself and Marie, carefully settling the kettle back on the coals. Nell had been up before him every morning since they left. He frowned, nodded to the others and returned to the lab, setting Marie's cup beside her.

"Have you seen Nell?"

Marie shook her head, not bothering to look up from the microscope. "Not yet. Did you check her tent?"

"I'll do that now." He put his cup down and strode quickly toward Nell's tent. He called Nell's name a few times outside the tent before letting himself in. His gaze went to her cot.

It was empty.

He went back out and jogged across to Scott's tent. Would she have gone in there for some reason? He poked his head in, but it was empty as well. Where could she be? And more importantly, why hadn't she told anyone she was leaving? He watched the pond for ripples that would indicate someone in the water, but the surface was still and quiet.

He went back by way of the fire. "Hey guys - come up to the lab tent. We need to talk." He waited to make sure they followed before he continued.

Marie glanced over her shoulder as everyone assembled around her and then turned with a frown. "What's going on?"

"Nell's missing." He watched all of their faces, not even really sure what he was looking for. A clue, maybe - something that would help explain her sudden disappearance.

Marie glanced over at Cynthia. "Was she in the tent when you left this morning?" The tech chewed nervously on her bottom lip as she looked at the ground.

"I wasn't exactly there," she admitted, stealing a quick look at Scott.

Frustration clouded Marie's face. "When was the last time you saw her?" Her voice was low and calm - scary calm as she waited for the answer.

"Last night," Cynthia murmured. She inched closer to Scott. Darren watched the other man's face closely. It wasn't longing on his face when he looked at her, but something closer to tolerance. Interesting in light of Cynthia's inferences. He turned back to Marie, still staring at the semi-happy couple. She looked like she couldn't decide whether to yell or cry. If only she'd lean on him - let him help.

He moved to stand beside her. "We need to keep going with the research," he said, holding a hand up when Marie started to protest. "It may be nothing - she may have just decided to go for a walk, or look for more specimens." He turned to Cynthia, her eyes moist with unshed tears. "You stay here and help Marie work. Scott and I will look around and try to figure out what might have happened. We'll meet back here in..." he looked down to check his watch. "...one hour. Is that okay with everyone?"

Scott and Cynthia nodded. Marie looked at him for a long moment, her eyes asking if she could trust him. Begging him not to betray her. He wanted to reassure her, tell her that everything would be okay, but he didn't know that it would. He could only hope that she saw something in him that she could believe in.

Finally, she nodded, and turned back to her work. Feeling as though something had just been ripped from him, Darren followed Scott outside, not daring to wonder where the search might lead.

* * *

The outside sounds and worry about Nell faded quickly as Marie went back to work. She was only somewhat aware of Cynthia working behind her as she checked, cataloged and tested again. She wasn't sure how long she'd been working when it all came together.

"My God - that's it!" She stepped back, staring at the table and her hastily written notes. It was so simple, why hadn't anyone found it before? Movement caught out of the corner of her eye reminded her she had company. "Cynthia, come here - look at this! We found it!"

"Found what?" She stepped up to the table, bending over the notes. Slowly she turned back to Marie, her brow furrowed.

Marie grinned. "Do you see it?"

"I think so..." Cynthia glanced over the papers again. "You realize what this means?"

She nodded. "We'll get all the funding we need, and more. And thousands of lives will be saved." She watched Cynthia's face. Where was the excitement? The happiness? "Are you okay?"

"Of course." Her assistant smiled, but it didn't quite seem sincere. "Would you just explain this last thing to me? I'm not sure I quite understand how it applies."

Marie moved forward, taking the papers with a frown. "Of course. If you look back here, you'll see that..."

A sharp thud reverberated through her head just before blinding pain blocked out any further thought. The world went black, and just before she passed out, she thought she heard two words.

"I'm sorry."

* **

"Marie? Marie, wake up!"

Hands pulled at her, and her head was throbbing. She wished they'd just go away, and leave her to sleep. So tired...

"Come on, honey - open your eyes."

She thought she heard Darren's voice. Did he call her honey? She tried to open her eyes, blinked once... then twice. God, that hurt.

"That's it. Look at me."

It was definitely Darren. She blinked her eyes again, finally forcing them to remain open. She found herself staring up into his worried gaze. "Ow," she grunted. Her mouth felt like cotton, and she swallowed, working her tongue to get the saliva flowing again. "Wh--what happened?"

"Looks like you got conked on the head - hard. Where's Cynthia?"

Marie glanced around, wincing at the movement. She looked back up at him, realizing that she was cradled in his arms. "I don't know. I showed her my notes - I'd just found the formula we needed and she asked me to explain something..."

"What happened next?" His voice was grim, and she closed her eyes, straining to remember what had happened just before she blacked out.

She opened her eyes, frustrated. "I'm sorry. She said something...I think she might have apologized. Did she knock me out?" She raised a hand to her forehead. "My head is killing me."

"I know." He hugged her closer for just a moment and then helped her sit up. "There's a pretty big bump on the back of your head. Looks like someone hit you with a flashlight. We found one on the ground next to you. Can you stand up?"

She nodded and winced again. "I think so." She allowed him to help her up, holding onto his shirt for support as the world seemed to spin around her. "Or maybe not. Can I sit for a minute?"

"Sure. There's a chair over here." He helped her to the chair and supported her while she lowered herself into it. "Scott, can you get her some water?"

She looked past Darren and saw Scott nod before he left the tent. Suddenly, she remembered why they'd been gone. "Nell - you were looking for Nell. Did you find her?"

"Yes." His voice was low, and he didn't look her in the eye. She knew something was wrong before he continued. "I think she was drugged. She was wandering around just north of camp, disoriented and groggy. She's resting on my sleeping bag now."

Marie turned her head slowly to peek under the table where he'd slept last night. Nell's form lay prone, the soft rise and fall of her chest the only indication she was alive. "Thank goodness you found her. Do you think she'll be okay? We need to get her to a hospital..."

"You could use a doctor yourself, but neither of you is in any shape to hike to the truck right now." He glanced down at Nell. "There's no way to tell what she was drugged with – we don't have the right equipment for that. We'll have to wait and see when it wears off. Her vital signs are good, so she's stable for now." Scott came back in with the water, and Darren took the bottle from him, holding it out to Marie. "Here, drink."

She took the bottle, tilting her head back and triggering another wave of dizziness. *So this was what a concussion felt like*, she silently mused as she took a long drink. "My notes are on the table over there - look at them. I found it - I found a compound that looks really promising to cure the flu virus." He walked over to the table, rifling through the contents. She frowned. Her notes were right on top - why couldn't he see them? He turned back to her, an apologetic look on his face.

"They aren't here, Marie." He went to the other table, and shuffled things around there. "They aren't here either. Did anyone besides Cynthia know about your findings?"

She shook her head, immediately regretting the action. "She's the only one. Are there any painkillers in the first aid kit?"

"I'll get them," Scott said, moving to the back corner of the tent. "Cynthia was the only one with you - the only one who knew about what you found. That makes her the most logical person to have knocked you out and taken your notes." He stood in front of her, dropping a couple of pills in her hand.

Darren nodded. "Yes, it does." He glanced behind him, and Marie followed his gaze. Nell was moving under the table, and he went to kneel beside her.

"Nell? Are you awake?"

Marie couldn't hear anything from her chair, but when she leaned forward with the intent to stand, the world started spinning again. She sat back and closed her eyes, focusing on the sounds around her. It was pretty quiet, with the occasional scuff of a foot on the dirt floor, and other people breathing. She could barely make out a whisper from the direction of Darren's bed, but couldn't quite hear the words. She opened her eyes again, resigned to waiting for a report. Darren was bent over Nell, apparently having a conversation with her. Marie wondered if her assistant's head felt as horrible as hers.

Finally, Darren came back. "She says the last thing she remembers is waking up, and seeing Cynthia standing beside her cot sometime last night." He rubbed his chin thoughtfully. "Either Cynthia is on Adams' payroll, or she intends to publish your findings herself. Is there enough information in the notes for her to do that?"

"Everything is there. She could publish the initial findings tomorrow if she could type that fast." She tried to push the feelings of betrayal back, focusing on what they could possibly do to solve the problem. "Is there any way to get to the truck before she does? That's the only way back to civilization."

Scott moved forward. "I could go for the truck...she doesn't have that much of a head start. I might be able to catch up or pass her."

"I don't think that's such a good idea," Darren said, a wary expression on his face. "You were pretty cozy with her. How do we know you're not in on it?"

Scott shrugged. "If I was in on it, would I be here with you guys? Why wouldn't I have taken you out and gone with Cynthia?"

"You both have a point, but I think Darren should go." Marie sat forward again, slowly. She waited for the spinning sensation, but it didn't come. Maybe the painkillers were helping. "Scott, you stay here with me, and once Nell is able to move again, you can help us get up to the valley entrance. Darren, bring the truck around, and if you happen to find Cynthia, get the papers from her." She rose from the chair, somewhat unsteady, but pushed away Darren's hand when he reached out to her. "Go now - she's already got a head start. We'll pack up a few things to take with us. I'll send a team out later to dismantle the camp."

He glanced at her one more time. "Marie, I--"

"Go!" She pointed toward the tent flaps. "We'll meet you at the entrance. Please. Just go."

He nodded and started to leave, stopping only to look Scott in the eye. "Take care of her." The other man nodded, and Darren left. She felt bereft the moment he walked out into the sunshine, hoping he found Cynthia in time to stop her.

***

Sweat ran down his face as Darren jogged through the trees, making his way back to the mouth of the hidden valley. He still wasn't sure leaving Marie and Nell with Scott was the best idea, but he hoped his instincts were right, and Scott wasn't in on Cynthia's plan. He fought a sense of betrayal himself - Cynthia had always been friendly, and always seemed like she wanted to help him out. Now it seemed obvious she'd only wanted a scapegoat.

He fought through a dense thicket of underbrush, and half-fell out into the opening at the valley's entrance. Stopping for a moment, he scanned the area. He had hoped he could catch Cynthia nearby, but all seemed quiet. He stayed close to the rock face, moving slowly as he walked back to the truck. He was almost around a huge boulder when he heard voices.

"You aren't going anywhere until you tell us where that box is, honey."

The tone was deep and gruff. Darren didn't recognize the speaker. He ducked behind the rock, peering out the other side as he tried to get a good view of the man. He slipped a small knife out of his pocket, silently berating himself for not bringing a better weapon.

"I told you - we took it to our camp. It's back in the valley. There's a team of scientists there - you can ask them." Cynthia's voice was shrill and panicked. He slid out from behind the rock, using a patch of tall bushes for cover as he inched closer.

"Then you'll just have to take us there."

Darren parted a few branches just enough to make a small peephole. There was a clearing just on the other side of the brush, and Cynthia stood on the far side facing two rough-looking men. The truck was still twenty yards behind her position. Maybe he could circle around and get to the truck. He closed the branches slowly, mindful not to make a sound. He crouched low and moved right, using the leafy curtain as cover.

"I--I can't go back. I sort of stole something."

The two men broke into laughter, and Darren took advantage of the brief noise to hurry to the cover of another large boulder. "No kidding. What did you steal - our box, maybe?"

"No...just some papers. I swear, your box is down in the valley at our camp."

Darren moved a few more feet, careful to watch his footing. He could see the red paint through the leaves just ahead.

"Enough."

Darren froze at the man's command, certain he'd been seen. He clutched the knife tightly, slowly turning to look over his shoulder. But he was still hidden, unable to see the men or Cynthia any longer.

"You're coming with us. Show us where your camp is, we'll get our stuff and be on our way. Go on - I will shoot you if you don't start walking."

"Okay, fine. I'm walking."

Darren covered the rest of the distance to the truck quickly, coaxing the door open just enough to climb into the cab. He left the door ajar and put the key into the ignition, and pressed the button to lower the window. He took a deep breath and fired up the engine. He shut the door and backed up, pressing the pedal down as he peeled forward and pulled up beside Cynthia.

"Get in," he called out the window, slowing beside her. She hesitated, a worried look on her face. "Come on!"

It was too late though. The younger man grabbed her arm and pulled her away from the truck. The other man raised his gun, and Darren had no choice but to press the gas pedal to the floor. The wheels spun on the loose top soil and kicked up a huge dust cloud as he drove toward the rendezvous point. Marie and Nell wouldn't be able to hike very fast, and he was pretty sure they wouldn't be waiting just yet.

It only took a couple minutes to reach the mouth of the valley. He scanned the area, not seeing any sign of the others. He parked at the other side of the entrance, striding back into the forest he'd left just an hour ago. If he could just get to them, warn them, maybe they could hide until the dealers went past.

Chapter Twelve

Breathing hard, Marie kept putting one foot in front of the other as she hiked up toward the mouth of the valley. She supported Nell on one side, and carried a bag full of samples and slides in the other. Scott walked on Nell's other side with her arm around his neck. The woman was barely conscious, and couldn't seem to regain her coordination for more than a few seconds at a time. Worried, Marie wondered what Cynthia had given Nell to knock her out for so long. Had she messed up the dosage? Or had she really intended to hurt or even kill Nell?

"Hang on." Scott stopped, pulling her and Nell to stop as well. He stood still for a moment, apparently listening as he turned in a full, slow circle. "I think someone's watching us."

Marie looked through the trees, her heart rate speeding up. She and Nell were in no shape to fight off a would-be attacker. She hoped it was just Scott's paranoia. She leaned across Nell, closer to him. "Do you see anything?" She kept her voice low and looked back over her shoulder, hoping who or whatever wouldn't sneak up from behind.

He shook his head, frowning. "Maybe it was nothing." He waited a few more seconds and then shrugged. "Let's keep going." He pulled them forward, and Marie did her best to keep up with his quicker pace. Her head throbbed again, and she felt so tired. She promised herself a nap when they got to the truck.

Off to the left, something darted between the trees.

"There!" She pointed, her throat tight as a man walked out of the woods towards them. When she recognized him, she frowned. "It's Darren. Why didn't he wait up there for us?"

"I'm glad I found you," he said, taking Nell's arm off her shoulder and placing it around his own. "We have to hide. Cynthia ran into the drug dealers on her way to the truck. They're forcing her to show them to the camp so they can get the drugs."

Marie glanced toward the valley entrance. "Why aren't we going to the truck? How are we going to help Cynthia?"

Darren led them into a small hollow in the cliff, hidden by tall, thick bushes and big boulders. He lowered Nell to the ground with Scott's help and then turned to Marie. "You and Nell couldn't move fast enough to beat them to the entrance," he said, his voice gentle. "If we hide here until they go by, we can get to the truck and be gone by the time they get back."

"But what about Cynthia? We can't just leave her out here with those guys..."

Darren looked at her, staring long and hard into her eyes. "She was - is stealing your work, Marie. Either to use herself, or sell to the highest bidder. Why should we care what happens to her?" His voice was rough with emotion, and she remembered that Cynthia had once been his friend.

Marie felt close to tears, blinking quickly to keep them at bay while her emotions warred inside. Yes, the woman had betrayed her, and in the worst possible way too. But she couldn't bring herself not to care. "I do care," she said, putting her hands on her hips. "We have to help her somehow."

"I have an idea." Scott helped Nell drink from a water bottle and capped it. "We can put Nell and Marie in the truck, and you and I can wait for them to come back through. When they go for their car, we can grab Cynthia and go. I can take the distributor cap off the car, so they can't follow us."

Marie nodded, watching Darren as he considered it. He didn't like the delay, she could tell. "It's not just Cynthia we'd be helping," she said finally. "I could get my notes back. That would help a lot."

"It's settled then." Scott gave them a forced smile, and went back to tending Nell. Marie watched him go, until Darren's touch on her arm sent another wave of awareness through her body.

She turned back just in time for his lips to descend over hers, his tongue playing at the seam of her lips as he pulled her close to his body. She leaned into him, putting up no resistance until a low moan from behind Darren pulled her out of the moment - and out of his arms. She peered around his arm and then pushed past him to go to Nell. She was waking up again.

"Nell, can you hear me?" She sat down by the woman, looking into her eyes when she blinked them open. The pupils weren't as dilated as they had been. "Your eyes look better - how do you feel?"

"Th-th-thirsty," she managed to croak out. Scott handed Marie a water bottle, and she held it to Nell's lips as she drank. "Thanks."

Handing the bottle back to Scott, Marie looked into Nell's face. "We're almost to the truck. We'll need to go soon. Think you can walk?"

Nell nodded. She looked over at Darren as he watched for the drug dealers through a deep crack in one of the boulders. "I'll try." She rubbed her eyes and then her forehead. "That was some drug. I feel like I've been trashed for a week."

"I know how you feel," Marie said, rubbing her neck. "She hit me on the back of the head."

"Time to go." Darren kept his voice low and motioned them over. He turned to Scott, a somber expression on his face. "They went just east and south of here. We'll head north and west. We need to move quickly."

Marie waited as the guys helped Nell up, and watched as the tech took a few tentative steps. "I think I'm okay, guys - thanks." She walked carefully over to Marie and turned back to raise an eyebrow at them. "Coming, boys?"

Darren nodded and then led the way out of their hiding spot. Marie followed, grateful to see the bright red of the truck just a few minutes later. She and Nell went straight for it as fast as they could. She pulled the door of the cab open and helped Nell climb up into the front seat. She hoisted herself up and then turned to Darren who had come up behind her.

"Where's Scott?" She craned her neck, trying to see through the reflections on the window glass.

Darren gestured vaguely in the other direction. "He went to disable their car." He pulled the rental key out of his pocket and handed it to her. "Here. If you hear shots, or if anything goes wrong, get the heck out of here."

"What, you mean like gunshots?" Marie fingered the key in her hand. "This is just way out of control. I never should have brought you all out here. I should have just left the school, found another lab, started over." She pulled her legs inside, and grasped the steering wheel, guilt washing over her cold and dark. "I'm so sorry for getting all of you in this mess..."

A warm hand slid over her thigh. "Hey." She looked back at Darren when he spoke. "It's not your fault. None of this is. Blame the school. Blame Riley Adams, or Cynthia, since she made that choice. It all just happened, and now we need to get out of it and get you back to the school so you can publish. Chin up, okay?"

She stared at him for a long minute and then nodded. "Okay." She took a deep breath, but couldn't quite return his gentle smile. Reaching out to grasp the door handle, she waited for him to move and then closed the door with a click. As he walked away, she wondered if things would ever be right again.

* * *

When Darren approached, Scott was just closing the hood on a dark blue muscle car that had seen better days.

"Everything okay?" he asked.

Scott nodded, holding up the distributor cap. "Yep - they aren't going anywhere now." He gestured for Darren to follow him around the side of the car. "I found something interesting back here too." He pointed in the back window and Darren bent down, cupping his hands on the glass and peering in. Sitting on the back seat was a burlap sack that looked very much like the one Marie had wrapped the first plant specimen in. He stood, frowning as he considered the implications.

"Did you look inside?"

Scott shook his head. "No, just noticed it on the way by. Think we should?"

Darren nodded, trying the door handle. It was open. Apparently the dealers - if that's who they really were - weren't worried about anyone stealing anything out here. He reached in and untied the twine holding the fabric together. It fell away, revealing the first plant he and Marie had retrieved. It was slightly wilted, but the bark underneath was still damp, keeping the roots plump and hydrated.

Scott leaned in, looking over his shoulder. "So they were the ones in camp the first night. It doesn't make sense. They took this, but not the box with their drugs? It's not like it was hidden or anything - we put it right in plain sight."

"That also means they didn't need Cynthia to show them where the camp was," Darren said, straightening. He ran a hand through his hair, looking out over the desert. "Unless Cynthia put the plant here when she saw the car. Maybe she thought it would be a convenient way to throw us off track." He turned back to the car, and wrapped the specimen back up. "We'll take this to Marie and then get Cynthia. Whatever's going on, we need to leave as soon as possible."

He waited while Scott tossed the electrical cables

into a bush several yards away and then they started towards the truck.

"I don't understand though - why would they take the plant?" Marie looked at him in confusion when Darren handed over the burlap package.

"We think Cynthia passed the car on her way out, and thought she'd frame them."

She nodded. "So, you two are going to ambush them, right?"

"That's the plan." He looked up at her, worry filling her beautiful eyes. He reached up and caressed her face through the open window. "I'll be back as soon as I can. Don't wait if you see them coming though - get out of here as fast as you can."

"I will."

He slid his hand down and walked away, following Scott through the trees.

* * *

"He's right, you know."

Marie started at the sound of Nell's voice half an hour later. She'd thought the other woman was asleep. She looked over to see Nell propped against the passenger door, her stare uncomfortably knowing. "Right about what?"

"It's not your fault that all this happened. Incredibly bad luck, maybe, but you couldn't have prevented any of it."

Marie shook her head. "Thank you, but you're

wrong. Maybe if I hadn't been so cold, Cynthia would have been more loyal. I wasn't a good friend to her." She looked back at Nell. "I'm not good with people. Not women, definitely not men. Maybe if I was--"

"Nah." Nell waved her off. "It wouldn't matter. Cynthia made her own choices. You could have been the warmest, friendliest person in the world, and she still would have stabbed you in the back. People like that don't care about anyone but themselves."

Marie gave her a slight smile. "Thanks. I don't believe you, but thanks."

"Besides, Darren is head over heels for you. Wouldn't give me the time of day." She looked down at her hands. "I'm sorry about that, by the way."

Marie stared out the windshield, at the barren landscape of the desert. "Why did you...approach him?"

"I don't know." She shrugged. "I think I was jealous of you - of him wanting you. It looked like you didn't want him, so I thought maybe..." She shrugged again. "It doesn't matter. He wants you - and you shouldn't let him get away. He's a good man. And seriously good-looking. You don't see that every day in our line of work."

Marie laughed. "No, I guess not. That's why I can't figure out why he'd be interested in plain ol' me." She picked at a loose thread beside her on the seat. "I'm nothing special."

"You are to him, and that's what matters, right?"

Nell winked.

She had to admit, the other woman had a point. "I guess so." She stared through the window, motion in the trees catching her attention. Could they have gotten all the way into the valley and back in such a short time? She put a hand on the key hanging in the ignition, and a foot over the gas pedal. She wanted to be ready when the others got back.

"What did you see?" Nell was leaning closer, peering over her shoulder to look out the window. "Are they back already?"

Marie shook her head. "It must have been my imagination," she said. "I don't see anything else...no, wait. There." She pointed out the window, just off to the left. "Did you see that?"

"Yes I did." Nell grabbed Marie's forearm, her grip tight. "Start the truck, Marie. Start it now."

Marie looked down at the hand gripping her arm and then up into Nell's face. She was white as a ghost. "What's wrong? What exactly did you see?"

"War paint," Nell whispered. "Are there natives here? Why haven't we seen them before?"

Marie turned the key, and the motor came to life with a deafening sound. "I don't know," she replied. "This is supposed to be public land, so I'm not sure why anyone would live out here." She left the sentence unfinished as several dark-skinned native-looking men dressed only in jeans and t-shirts stepped out of the underbrush. Each had a large, intricate tattoo covering both sides of his neck and a large hunting knife strapped to his belt; but it was the long, curved machete each of them held that made Marie's blood run cold.

"Drive." Nell was practically bouncing in the seat beside her. "Go. Drive!"

Marie shifted the transmission into drive, hesitating even as the natives started to advance. "But what about the others? We can't leave them here!"

"We can't protect ourselves from these guys. Darren and Scott can take care of themselves. We'll come back for them later - we have to go, Dr. Simco."

"I know." She lowered her foot to the pedal and drove off, seeing one of the men raise his arm just before the tires kicked up a big cloud of dust. "And you can call me Marie." She drove off away from the valley, away from the cliffs and across the open desert toward the highway. She checked the rear view mirror, but no one followed, and she breathed a sigh of relief. "What now?" she asked, not really expecting an answer.

"I'd say it's time to bring in the police, don't you think?"

She glanced at Nell and then back to the landscape ahead. "I guess so." She pulled onto the highway, and floored the gas, heading for the nearest town to get help.

Chapter Thirteen

Darren motioned for Scott to stay in his position on the far side of the pond. They'd decided to go all the way back to camp and ambush the drug dealers there. Tied up, the drug dealers could remain at the camp while Darren and Scott went for help with the women. They had split up, each coming at the camp from a different angle and Darren had just seen movement from the lab tent that could indicate where the dealers were now. He moved forward silently, pretending he was a soldier in one of those action flicks who had to save a hot chick from certain death. Unfortunately, he was saving someone who was stealing from the hot chick he wanted, but he tried not to think about that.

Raised voices reached him as he used the girls' tent for cover, moving quickly behind it and then running for the lab tent. He crouched low behind an area where he knew there was a table on the other side, hoping no one would see his shadow on the inside of the canvas. Then he signaled for Scott to move in.

"Please - don't kill me." Cynthia's pleading voice rose loudly in the late afternoon air. "I gave you your drugs - just let me go, and I won't say a thing. I just really need to get out of here."

"Now honey, you know we can't do that. You've seen our faces. I'm afraid we can't just let you walk away, that's not how this works. Don't you watch TV?" Darren recognized the scratchy voice of the older man speaking as Scott moved into position on the other side of the tent.

Cynthia was sobbing, her cries making enough noise to cover their entrance. Darren held a hand out to Scott, with three fingers up. He lowered one, and then another, and when the third dropped, they sprang up and ran into the tent, each tackling one of the men as Cynthia looked up in surprise.

The older man had been on Darren's side of the tent, and he went down hard, squeezing off a shot as he went. Darren didn't have time to see where the bullet had gone, but knew he was outmatched as they rolled around on the floor. He did his best to keep the upper hand, but in the end, found himself knocked to the ground, the man straddling his ribs and gripping his throat in a chokehold. He grabbed the man's wrists, trying to pry them away but the angle was wrong, and he was running out of air quickly. He started flailing his arms and legs, trying to hit or kick anything that would make a difference as he felt the fog starting to fall over his brain.

Just as he was about to black out, the other man jerked up before falling over beside Darren. Cynthia stood over him with a microscope in her hand. She must have hit the dealer on the head. He gulped air back into his lungs, immediately turning to look for Scott and his foe. They were on the other side of the tent, but apparently Scott was a better fighter, because the younger dealer was bound and unconscious in a chair while Scott finished tying off the rope. He sat up, looking around for Cynthia, who had disappeared. Then he saw her a few feet away, sprawled on her back in the dirt.

"Cynthia?" He crawled to her, taking in the blood pooling underneath her as she lay there. More blood came from a hole in her upper chest. He bunched up her shirt over the wound, pressing hard against it, but he knew it was too late when a stream of blood and foamy pink bubbles formed at her mouth. Her lips moved, and he bent down, trying to make out her last words.

"Tell Marie...I'm sorry," she whispered. He nodded, and watched as her head fell back, her last breath coming out in a sigh. He reached up and closed her eyes before retrieving Marie's papers from her pocket. He sat back, glancing over to see Scott securing the older drug dealer's hands and ankles with rope. When he finished, he came over and held a hand out to help Darren up, barely looking at Cynthia.

Darren reached up and squeezed Scott's shoulder. "I'm sorry it didn't work out." Scott nodded, turning away. Darren noticed the hard look in the other man's eyes and knew it would be a while before Scott would trust another woman. "We should bury her. There won't be anything left of the body when we get back otherwise."

Scott shook his head. "There isn't time. We have to get out of here before those two wake up. Leave her there."

"I'll take her body outside, at least. We don't want whoever comes back to stumble on it." Darren bent down, slipping his hands under her. He picked her up, struggling under the weight now that her body was fully limp. "Bring some of that rope and a tarp - I have an idea."

He carried her out to a large, tall tree several yards away from camp. "We'll wrap her up, and hoist her into the tree. That should keep the body safe from animals, at least." Scott helped him tie the tarp securely around her. Darren tossed the rope up over a branch and both men pulled the body up. Darren pulled the rope taut around the trunk and tied it off at shoulder height. When they were done, they both stood back and looked at the macabre bundle hanging down. Darren turned away, feeling queasy.

"Let's go," Scott said, leading the way out of the

camp and back up the now familiar path to the entrance.

* * *

"Halt."

Scott skidded to a stop, and Darren nearly ran into him as they looked around, trying to figure out where the command had come from. Scott turned in a circle, listening and watching for any sound or movement.

"Show yourself," Darren called, frowning. There was no way the drug dealers could have gotten free so quickly, and he hadn't recognized the voice.

Scott slapped Darren's arm with the back of his hand. "There - through those trees." He pointed, and Darren leaned in to look. "See him?"

"I don't..." Darren squinted, moving a little closer for a better view. "Wait - yeah, yeah I see him." He straightened. "We can see you - who are you? What do you want with us?"

"You have something that belongs to us."

Darren jumped at the words spoken right behind him, whirling around with Scott right next to him as the adrenaline flew through his body. A tall, dark-skinned tattooed man in jeans and an old white t-shirt stood staring at them, a large machete in hand.

"Return the plants and you may leave."

"We don't have any plants." Scott held his hands out to the side, palms up. "You've got the wrong people. Now if you'll excuse us, we really need to..."

He took a step to the side, only to be stopped by another native blocking his path. He backed up again.

Darren tilted his head to the side, curious. "I'm Dr. Darren Newbury. I'm here with a scientific team led by Dr. Marie Simco. Our research was approved by the tribal leaders who made the medicine in this valley known to us. Who are you?"

"I am Anjou. We protect this valley and its secrets from the outside world. The plants are the tree dwelling species your team has so crudely carved from their homes among the branches – a practice I'm sure was not approved. They are not yours to take, nor ours to give. You must return them - they belong here."

Darren nodded, frowning at the forest floor. "I see. We have a problem then." From the corner of his eye he saw the man on their right raise another machete. "Dr. Simco has the plants in the truck at the mouth of the valley. But I'm sure if we go speak to her, we can work something out. Will you come with us?"

"That's not possible." The native gave a subtle nod to his companions, and they relaxed their stances. "The women drove off when we approached them. So the plants have left the valley." He looked up at the sky. "This is not good. We must get them back to return the balance." He lowered his head, and fixed his gaze back on Darren. "How can we contact these women?"

He held the man's stare. "We can't," he said. "They'll come back though - they won't leave us stranded out here. We'll have to wait for them."

Scott shifted uneasily. "What about the guys back at camp?"

Darren shrugged, glancing over at the photographer. "How long do you think the bonds will hold?"

"I can send men to take care of them," Anjou said. "We watched them sneak into your camp the other night, and scared them away when they would have entered your sleeping quarters."

Darren looked at him in surprise. "Thank you, but why, when you thought we were stealing your plants?"

"The tribal leaders always make it clear when people request access to our resources that nothing can be removed from the valley. There are harvesting guidelines given out as well. Your leader should know all of this."

Darren remembered that Cynthia had made most of the arrangements for the trip. Apparently she'd left out a few key details when relaying the information to Marie. "We weren't aware that we couldn't remove the plants from the valley," he said truthfully. "Our intention was to grow them in a lab, to mass-produce medicine."

Anjou shook his head, his expression grave. "If you were to take the plants away from this place, they would not survive. People have tried in the past. That is why we've been given the task to protect them, and ensure they remain here. In order for the plants to survive and reproduce, they must be in this environment."

"Do you live out here?" Scott asked, glancing at the two other men. "By yourselves?"

"All city tribal members are given the choice to volunteer for this duty when they turn twenty-five. When we are sixty-five, we must rejoin society, and let a younger member take our place."

Scott shook his head. "So you spend forty years out here, protecting plants and then you have to go back to the city. That must be some serious culture shock."

Anjou smiled. "It's not so bad to come here from there. It's the transition back that is difficult." He gestured to the other men, who joined him. "Dr. Newbury, do you understand the importance of returning the plants to this valley as soon as possible?"

"Yes sir - I think I do. But the medicine they hold is very powerful - is there no way to produce it outside the valley, so many people can benefit from it?"

"I'm not sure." Anjou lowered his head, studying the ground thoughtfully. "Do you know which part of the plant contains the compound that you speak of?"

Darren shook his head. "Marie was the one who figured it out - she would have to tell you."

"Excuse us for just one minute," Anjou said, pulling his companions off to the side. They bent their heads together, murmuring for a few seconds. He turned back to Darren. "I trust that you are a man of honor, Dr. Newbury. If you bring the women and those plants back to us, I believe we can find some sort of compromise to make the compound available to you."

"Normally, I'd take you up on that," Darren said, feeling sheepish. "But the truck was our only transportation. We're stranded out here until they come back."

Anjou grinned. One of the other men pulled out the distributor cap that Scott had taken off the old muscle car that the drug dealers were driving. "I believe there is one alternative," he said, holding the part out to Scott.

Darren smiled back. "Thank you. We'll be back as soon as we can. The men in our camp..."

"They'll be well taken care of." As if on cue, the two other men turned and walked into the forest in the direction of the camp, fading away without even a whisper of sound. "Hurry - there isn't much time before the plants wilt and die."

* * *

"Is this the right place?" Marie looked out the window at the dilapidated old house on main street that boasted an equally run down wooden sign with "Police" simply carved into the front. She'd stopped at the first town they'd come to on the old highway, and asked the waitress at the diner for directions to the police station. Now, she wondered if they'd made the right choice.

Nell looked down at her notes. "The address is right - I guess there's only one way to find out." She looked up at Marie with one eyebrow raised.

Marie nodded. "How'd you learn how to do that?" she asked as she reached for the door handle.

"Do what?"

Nell got out, and Marie slid out as well and walked around the truck to meet her. "The eyebrow thing - how do you raise one without the other?"

Nell grinned as they walked up the stairs, standing in front of a run-down wooden door that didn't look like it could keep anyone out. She rapped on the door firmly with her knuckles. "Contest with my little brother when I was eight," she said. "My uncle taught him, and he bet me a whole dollar I couldn't learn how in one afternoon. I spent the next three hours in front of a mirror."

Marie laughed. "Amazing how motivating a dollar was back then, isn't it?"

The door opened, and they both turned to find and older man in jeans and a plaid button down shirt staring at them. "Yes?" he said, stepping back and motioning for them to come in. "What can I do for you ladies?"

"We have a little problem," Marie said. "We just came from the Oasis Valley out in the desert, and there were natives that came after us, so we had to leave the rest of my team there. They were going after drug dealers who basically kidnapped my lab assistant." She paused for a breath, noting the confusion and disbelief on the man's face. "I'm sorry - I should have asked if this was the police station first."

He grunted, glancing around the room. "You saw the sign outside, right?"

Marie nodded, noting the curved wooden counter they were standing in front of for the first time. She smiled apologetically. "Yes, sorry. I didn't mean to--"

"Is this some kind of joke?" The man went behind the counter and leaned on its worn surface. "Because I really do have real work to take care of today."

Marie sighed. "Sir, I really wish this was a joke. I came out here with a team of scientists to do research in Oasis Valley. All I wanted was to find out what was so special about the Mawai plant, and publish my results so I could keep the funding for my lab. But we have to go back, and we need your help. If you won't help, I'll drive to the next town." She paused, waiting for his reply.

"You had a run-in with the natives in Oasis Valley?"

She nodded, relieved he was at least going to hear her out. "Yes. We were in the truck, getting ready to leave with three men started toward us. One had a bow and arrows, the second a spear, and the third a machete. We got scared and left before the rest of my team could join us."

"Must have been Anjou - I think he's the leader up there now." He tilted his head at her, curiosity in his eyes. "Why did you run? They wouldn't have hurt you. They just protect the plants and animals in the valley." He thought for a moment, his brows drawing together. "Did you take anything when you left? Anything that was originally in the valley?"

Marie shrugged. "Just a few plants - the reason I went there was to collect samples to take back to the lab..." she grew quiet as he shook his head slowly.

"That explains it," he said, glancing from her to Nell and back. "Removing any plant or animal life from the valley is strictly forbidden. Many of the living things there are believed to have magical or healing powers - and to remove them from that environment is said to diminish or remove the properties that make them special. Something in the water, maybe."

Marie shared a confused look with Nell. "But we had permission to be there - to research the Mawai plant and look for a cure for the flu."

"Sure," the man said. "They give everyone permission who asks to go there. You just can't take anything out with you when you go. I'm surprised they didn't tell you that."

She tried to remember a conversation with the tribal leaders. She realized she hadn't been the one to speak with them and turned to Nell again. "Cynthia set everything up.'"

"That explains a lot," Nell commented.

Marie sighed, looking back at the man. "I'm sorry, what's your name? I'm Dr. Marie Simco, and this is Dr. Carson."

"Andrew Jakes, at your service."

Marie offered her hand, pleased when he didn't try to squeeze hers in his grip. "Officer Jakes-"

"Andrew." He grinned.

Marie forced a return smile. "Andrew. So if we return the plants, that will take care of the problems with the natives, right?"

"Yes ma'am. What was your other problem?"

She shook her head. "When we rented the truck in Albuquerque, there was a small box in the back. We didn't find it until later - and when we opened it, we found a bag of drugs. I was in a hurry to get to the valley, so we kept going. Somehow, the people the drugs belong to followed us there. They kidnapped my lab assistant, and my other two team members went after her. They're still in the valley."

"Hmm." Andrew rubbed his chin. "I guess I'll be coming out with you then. Let me just call my deputy, and have him come over. I'll feel better with a little back-up for something like this."

Marie nodded. "Thank you so much, Andrew. I can't tell you how much I appreciate this." She looked around, finally realizing that they were back in civilization. "Do you...uh...have a restroom I could use?"

"Down the long hall, last door on the left."

* * *

An hour later, Marie got back into the truck and followed a beat-up Bronco onto the highway. Nell had opted to ride with Andrew and his deputy, who had turned out to be a very hot younger guy that Nell had immediately drooled all over. He hadn't seemed to mind, and Marie was content to drive back alone. She wondered why she'd never really talked to Nell much before. They were actually a lot alike, it seemed, and she decided that when they got back, she'd make a point of spending more time getting to know her colleagues.

The miles slipped away quickly, and it wasn't long before the imposing rock cliffs rose up out of the desert again. Nerves took up residence in her stomach as they reached the turnoff and started across the soft sand to the oasis entry. She frowned as a rusted blue car came toward them in a cloud of desert dust. Had the plan gone horribly wrong? That had to be the car that the drug dealers had driven - the one that Scott was supposed to disable.

Several scenarios ran through her head of what might have happened, none of them good. She was somewhat reassured to see Andrew turn his lights on, and pull in front of the car to stop it. She coasted to a stop, watching as he exchanged words with the driver through the car window. When the car pulled away, it turned and headed back toward the valley. She followed Andrew to the entrance, parked beside his Bronco and swung the door open. Her feet were barely on the ground when Darren appeared, his hands grabbing her waist and lifting her out into his embrace.

She went willingly, wrapping her arms around his neck. Thank goodness he was okay. He pulled back enough to look into her face, a small smile touching his lips. "Are you okay?"

She laughed. "Am I okay? Of course - the question is, are you okay? What happened? Did you get Cynthia?"

"I'm afraid not," he said, his eyes sad as they looked into hers. "Marie...she didn't make it."

She shook her head. "I don't understand - she's dead? What happened? How?"

"I'll go over it with you later." She opened her mouth to protest, but he silenced her with his fingers pressed to her lips. "Later. I promise. Right now, we need to get those plants back into the valley, and see what kind of a compromise Anjou came up with while we were gone."

"Ahem." Andrew came around the side of the truck, and Darren stepped back, releasing her from his hold. Marie felt the heat rise in her face again, feeling strangely bereft without the support of Darren's arms. "Are we ready to head in?"

Marie nodded, and turned back to the truck. "Just let me get my bag - the plants are in it." She climbed up, more aware of her butt sticking out than she should have been, and retrieved her bag from the back seat. She scrambled down, trying to regain her dignity as she shut the door and willed her professional self to come forward. This wasn't the time to be mooning over a lab tech, or worrying about what certain parts of her anatomy looked like. She had to focus.

Andrew walked past them into the trees as if he knew exactly where to go. Marie followed, avoiding Darren's gaze and nodding to Scott, Nell and the deputy as they fell in behind. She knew he wouldn't understand, but she wasn't sure how else to get control of herself, so she hoped he'd let her explain later. Right now, they had to meet with this Anjou and get the plant thing figured out. It seemed like all her planning and the work they'd done was in vain if they wouldn't be allowed to use the results after all.

She glanced back at Darren, remembering her notes. "Did you happen to get my notes from Cynthia before..."

He nodded. "They're right here." He took several folded sheets of paper out of his pocket, and handed them to her.

"Thank you." She tucked the pages away, trying to ignore the small reddish brown stain on the corner and what it meant. She turned forward again, and nearly ran into Andrew when he stopped abruptly. The native man she'd seen before stood before them.

Chapter Fourteen

"Sheriff Jakes." Anjou shook the sheriff's hand before turning toward Marie. "And you must be Dr. Simco. Pleased to meet you." He took her hand as well, giving it a brief shake. "Might I ask - did you bring the Mawai plants back?"

She nodded. "They're right here." Darren watched as she put her bag on the ground and crouched before it, taking out the three burlap parcels that contained her specimens.

She stood and handed them to Anjou, who gave her a half-bow in thanks. "I'm sorry we took these - I was under a mistaken assumption that we were permitted to do so." She hesitated and then continued. "If there is any way we could get a few samples to take back, or even just the compounds, that would be so helpful, and it could save thousands of lives."

"Mashi will make sure these are returned to their

homes." Anjou handed the plants off to another nat-ive, who ran into the forest with them. "Would it be possible, Doctor, for you to show me your tests, and explain to me exactly what you want to do with these...ah...compounds?"

Marie nodded. "Certainly. If you'll come back to the camp with us, I'd be happy to tell you whatever you want to know about the project." She smiled, and Darren was struck again by her natural beauty. He wondered if he'd ever be able to convince her she was beautiful.

Andrew turned to him as they started hiking to-ward the camp. "The lady mentioned something about drug dealers? You know anything about that?"

"Unfortunately, sir. Scott and I ambushed them at our camp, but the woman we were trying to save got shot by one of them in the process. We tied them up and left them down there - Anjou said he'd make sure they were taken care of, whatever that means."

"I guess we'll see," the sheriff replied. "And the woman who got killed - she was part of your team?"

Darren nodded. "Cynthia. She'd stolen Dr. Simco's research notes, and was trying to leave so she could sell them off when the drug dealers caught her." He paused, making sure Marie was out of earshot before continuing. "As much as I'd like to pin it on those drug guys, her death was accidental. Scott and I attacked, and I got the guy with the gun. I knocked him down while he had his finger on the trigger."

"Noted," Andrew said. "Not that it will matter much. We take drug problems pretty seriously around here, and if Anjou's guys got to them first, no telling what they're tripping on by now. Some natural hallucinogen, no doubt. Anjou's boys are amused at the effects hallucinating has on people.

Darren's lips tugged up at the corners. He could just imagine those two going crazy from the images in their heads. Interesting punishment, but fitting, and apparently carried out rather quickly. Then he remembered that they'd left the men in the lab tent. "I hope they don't break anything - there's some very expensive equipment in the tent. "

Andrew waved off his concerns. "Don't worry about it. I'm sure they've been moved to more suitable accommodations."

* * *

Darren saw what the sheriff meant when they entered the camp twenty minutes later. Two primitive cages made from what looked like sapling trunks bound together with thick vines each contained one of the men. They were sitting on the ground, rocking back and forth.

Anjou looked back at the group, a wide grin on his face. "We gave them a tea made from ingredients only found in the valley. In the short term, it gives hallucinations and a poor general feeling. When it wears off, any narcotic they attempt to take will be immediately rejected by their bodies."

"Wow," Nell said, stepping forward. "If this flu thing doesn't work, maybe we should try marketing that."

Marie held up a hand. "One thing at a time, please. We don't even know if we can publish our findings yet." She looked at Anjou, and pointed to the lab tent. "Would you like to come with me, and I can show you what we've been doing?"

"Of course," he said, following her across the camp.

Darren started to follow, but stopped when he saw the sheriff take note of the blood trail away from the camp. He joined the man beside the tree, pointing up. "We didn't know what to do with the body, so we put it up there to keep it away from the animals."

"We'll need to bring it down," the sheriff said, motioning for his deputy to join them. "The body is evidence in a crime." He turned to the deputy. "Head back to the truck - get the rescue cage and a body bag. Take that guy with you." He pointed to Scott, who nodded and left with the deputy.

Now," he said, looking back down at the blood trail, "I need to see where this struggle happened, and I'll need those drugs for evidence."

"Sure thing. Follow me." Darren led the way up to the lab tent, where they joined Marie and Anjou, who were bent over a microscope, and barely acknowledged them. "The drugs are here." He pulled the white box from the corner and set it on the back table. He opened the latches, and swung the top open, frowning.

Andrew leaned closer, peering into the empty box. "I take it they were here?"

"This is the box we found them in - I don't know why anyone would have moved them." He turned toward the other two. "Marie - did you move the bag of drugs?"

She straightened and walked over to look down into the empty box. "No. Did you ask Nell or Scott?"

"I think they both went to get some things from the truck with the deputy." He ran a hand through his hair, letting out a long breath. "I'm sorry, Sheriff - apparently, we don't have a clue what's going on around here."

Andrew looked around the tent, and Darren knew he must be wondering what kind of scientists kept such a messy work space. Everything was askew, his sleeping bag and Marie's were pulled half out from under the tables, and there was the dark spot in the center of the tent where Cynthia's blood had seeped down into the earth. He shook his head, amazed at how the order they'd had at one point had become so corrupted.

"How well do you know the other two - Nell and Scott?"

Darren shrugged, glancing at Marie. "I just joined

the team right before we came out here, and the only person I really knew well...or thought I did, was Cynthia."

"You really think one of them has something to do with the missing drugs?" Marie's eyes were shiny, and Darren knew she was holding back tears. It was bad enough that one team member had been involved in a betrayal of trust, but someone else too? He took a step towards her, but she stepped back, giving him a slight head-shake. It hurt that she'd rather face this on her own than accept his support.

"We have to explore every possibility." Andrew turned back to Darren. "There are two other tents - I assume those are sleeping quarters?" Darren nodded. "I'll need to search them."

Darren glanced at Marie, who nodded. He gestured for the sheriff to join him, and walked to the front of the tent. "Come on, I'll show you."

* * *

Marie was tense as Darren and Andrew left to search the other tents. She tried to focus on the research she was showing Anjou, but realized her hand was shaking when his dark hand closed softly over hers to steady the slide she'd been holding.

"You are troubled," he said, his voice kind.

She looked up into his eyes, full of compassion. "I'm sorry," she said, looking away to control the emotion welling up in her. "This thing with my team -

I don't know how to deal with it. I thought I could trust these people..."

He patted her hand and then withdrew his. "You can't allow this to make you close yourself off to people, Dr. Simco." He held up a hand when she would have protested. "I saw you step back from Dr. Newbury when he would have given you support. You must not allow this to taint your other relationships. You can't control other people's actions, but you can control how much power they have in your own life."

She gave a small laugh, wiping at a tear that had escaped down her cheek. "You don't know me. I've been shutting people out for a long time. It's who I am." She looked up at him with a sad smile, touched that he wanted to help. "And just when I decide to start letting people in, this happens. What am I supposed to think?"

"Exposing yourself will always result in more hurt; it's true." He grinned. "But it also results in greater joy, and that makes the risk worthwhile."

She shrugged. "I'm still not sure it does," she said, taking a deep breath. She turned back to the slides, eager to refocus her thoughts on work. "So what do you think - is there any way I can make this marketable outside of this valley? Or is the cure destined to remain locked up here for eternity?"

"Well," he scratched his head, apparently staring at something over her shoulder. "The plant won't exist outside the valley. There's no way to recreate this exact environment for it, even in a lab. Others have tried before, and failed. But it seems as though you've grown the compound here in your little jars..." he indicated the Petri dishes she had set up along the back of the table, "and if you can keep it growing in this solution, could you create your cure from that?"

She considered the samples for a moment. "Maybe. I haven't done much with synthetic drugs - I prefer to use them in their natural state as much as I can. But in this case, it seems I have no choice." She looked back up at him. "Is it okay if I come back, and do some more testing on the Mawai plants as long as I leave them where I find them? It would help to find out exactly how the different compounds in the plant work together. Then I would know better how to recreate it in the lab."

"Of course." He looked thoughtfully at her. "Maybe I could persuade the tribal members to allow you a certain amount of seed to take with you. If you can get them growing, you could study what it might be in the environment that is so crucial to their health. It would be nice to know that this valley isn't the only place that can support them - that if anything ever happens here, they could be saved."

Marie grinned. "That sounds like a wonderful solution." She held out her hand to him, and he enfolded it in his. "Thank you, Anjou for helping us. I'll be sure to acknowledge your help in my paper."

"Thank you, but that's not necessary." He frowned, and she wondered what she'd said wrong. "This paper - will it mention the valley?"

"Yes, of course - why?" As soon as the words were out of her mouth, Marie realized his worries. "You're afraid more people will come, and things will get out of control." He nodded. "I see the problem," she said. "I'll do my best to keep the location of the valley secret. It would hurt my research just as much as yours to have more people stomping around."

He inclined his head. "Thank you." He looked around the tent. "Will you be leaving now, or will you stay for more research?"

"Unfortunately, I have to get back and publish my findings as soon as possible." She sighed, rubbing her forehead with one hand. "If I don't get funding, none of this matters. I can't afford to go forward alone. I'll need a new team too, and more equipment..."

"Marie?" She turned, the sound of Darren's voice surprising her. "I think you should come see this."

* * *

She glanced at Anjou and then followed Darren out of the tent and toward the men's tent. "Did you find the drugs?"

He nodded. "It looks like Scott took them - they were in his bag." He held the tent flap back and waited for her to enter ahead of him. The sheriff was standing in front of a cot, the contents of a duffel bag spread out in front of him.

"Why?" Marie asked, staring down at the bag sitting near the center of the pile. "What was he going to do with them?"

"Sell 'em." Scott spoke from the entrance to the tent, and they all turned as one to look at him. "My plan was to sell them back to the dealers for a higher price. Call it a ransom. But the actual drugs are gone. Taste that."

The sheriff flicked out a pocket knife and made a short cut in the bag. He took a small sample out on the blade, and held it up to his nose. He put a tiny amount on his tongue, frowning. "What is this?"

"I found a mineral deposit near that waterfall that dumps into the pond." Scott smiled, clearly proud of himself. "They looked pretty similar, so I substituted the minerals for the drugs. I was going to put that back in the box, but then you to decided to sleep in the lab, and I couldn't get access."

The sheriff stood, shaking his head. "It's a good thing you didn't get very far. Dealers aren't stupid. You would have been killed." He walked toward Scott. "So where are the drugs now?"

"I buried them." Scott shrugged, pointing vaguely north. "Somewhere out that way. I didn't really pay much attention since I didn't plan on going back."

"So, let me see if I have this straight," Andrew rubbed his neck with one hand, staring out across the pond. "We have drug dealers, but no drugs to implic-

ate them with. A shooting that was apparently accidental, with a body up in a tree. Research secrets that
were stolen, but recovered with no ill effects - at least
not to the owner. And stolen property from a public
valley that has been returned, again with no lasting ill
effects." He turned back to look at them, and Marie
slowly nodded. "Aside from dealing with a body,
what am I doing here? You all seemed to have resolved everything just fine without me so far..."

"But what about the drug dealers?" Marie stepped
forward, though her voice cracked a little. "Aren't you
going to take them to jail? Even without the drugs,
they still shot Cynthia..."

"Honey, Dr. Newbury here says that was an acci-
dent." He glanced over at Darren. "Care to refute
that?" Darren shook his head. "From what you all
say, that girl had just stolen important documents
from you. Not a jury in the world that would feel
sorry for her, or convict them for that. And without
those drugs..." He shook his head and walked out of
the tent. Marie followed, aware of Scott and Darren
behind her. The deputy was lowering Cynthia's body
onto the rescue cage while Nell held it steady. Darren
and Scott went over to help, the sheriff remaining at
Marie's side.

"She doesn't have any family," Marie remarked
offhand. "I wish I knew why she did it."

"It's always either money or fame, in my experience," Andrew said. "But sometimes we never find

out which." Darren and Scott walked by, hauling the rescue cage with Cynthia's body between them toward the mouth of the valley. The deputy stopped in front of the sheriff, wiping sweat from his face with his arm. "What else?"

He glanced back at the cages, and the two men who were finally looking more coherent. "You can cuff those two, we'll take 'em in and hold them for twenty-four hours and then explain to them why they need a new business model."

The deputy tipped his hat and walked toward the cages, and the sheriff looked at Marie. "If I were you, I'd pack up and get out of here, at least for a while. Go back home and get things in order. This place ain't going anywhere."

She nodded. "Thank you, Andrew. I'm sorry we caused you so much trouble."

"Nonsense." He raised two fingers to the brim of his hat as the deputy brought the drug dealers over in cuffs. "Haven't had this much excitement in a while - does a body good every so often." They left, and Marie and Nell started packing up supplies.

Chapter Fifteen

The sun was setting and Darren looked down at his watch, surprised to see that it was nearly eight in the evening. He glanced around at the group, taking in the exhaustion on all of their faces. Anjou had disappeared, it seemed, along with his companions, and all the pressing problems seemed to be resolved.

"It's getting late," he said, breaking the silence that had fallen over their group. "I think we should eat and get some sleep. We can pack up and move out in the morning."

Nell stepped forward. "I'll go get some meal packs." She looked over at Scott. "Want to start a fire for us?" They walked off, leaving Darren and Marie alone for the moment.

He moved closer, reaching out to grab her arm gently when she started to move away. "Come here," he said, pulling her into his arms. He held her close, rocking gently back and forth until she finally snuggled against his chest, wrapping her arms around his waist. Her shoulders shook, and he realized she was crying. He kissed her head, holding her until the tears dried up and she pulled back, her face red.

"I'm sorry," she said quietly, digging a tissue out of her pocket to wipe her nose. "I didn't mean to cry all over you." She dropped her gaze. "And now I'm a mess - how embarrassing."

He grinned, tilting her head up with a finger under her chin. "You're beautiful. And you needed to let it out." He leaned in, pressing a chaste kiss on her lips. "Feel better?" She nodded.

"A little." A crackling sound behind them had her turning, and he followed her gaze to the fire Scott had started. "Should we go sit down?"

He nodded, and reached out to lace his fingers with hers. "Sure, let's go." He walked with her to the fire, and Nell brought MRE packs, handing one out to each of them. They ate in silence as darkness fell around them, and he thought of how different this night was from their first one in the valley just a few days ago.

"So what's next, Marie?" Nell set her meal tray aside, and hugged her knees to her chest. "Do you have enough to publish when we get back?"

Marie nodded. "I think so. The research is sound, and there's a good chance we can develop an actual cure with the knowledge we've gained here, even if we end up having to grow it in the lab." She scooted a little closer to the fire, and Darren took the opportunity to move a little closer to her. "I don't know what Adams has been up to while we we've been gone, so I guess whether we get the money just depends on what kind of a project he developed in the meantime."

"So I still have a job then?" Nell grinned, and Marie smiled back.

"If you still want it."

Darren couldn't resist touching her any longer. He reached out a hand to rub lightly over her shoulders. "What about me," he asked softly. "Do I still have a job when we get back?"

She glanced at him over her shoulder, a mixture of fear and something else in her eyes. "I'm still thinking about that," she said coyly. Was she flirting with him? He grinned.

"I think that's our cue to leave." Scott stood and winked at Darren as he helped Nell to her feet. "You two have a good night - see you in the morning."

"Good night," Marie said, watching them walk away. Darren leaned back against a log, tugging at Marie's shirt until she lay back next to him, his arm under her shoulders and her head on his chest. "I really should go get some sleep," she said, one hand resting on his chest. He could feel how tense her muscles were against him. She was nervous.

He ran a finger down the side of her face, smiling

at the way she refused to look up at him. "Relax," he said, tracing the side of her neck and then the collar of her shirt. "Everything's going to work itself out." He stroked his fingers through her hair, looking up at the stars twinkling above as he felt her breathing slow. "You'll publish your paper, get your funding, and everything will be okay." He looked back down at her, stroked a hand down her face once more. "You really are beautiful, you know."

A little snore escaped her lips. He held her close, enjoying the feel of her warm breath across his chest as she slept. The fired died down, and when she shivered, he carefully stood, slipped his arms underneath her and carried her up to the lab tent. She woke as he was setting her in the chair, a small protest passing her lips.

"Shh. Just sit here a minute." He made sure she was secure in the chair and got both of their sleeping bags, spreading one out flat on the ground near the back of the tent. Unzipping the other, he placed it on top and connected them together, leaving one side open. He removed his shoes and her own, picked her up, and laid her in the makeshift bed, lowering himself beside her. Tucking the cover around them, he pulled her tightly against his body. She sighed, and turned in his arms, her fingers caressing the side of his neck.

"Darren." He looked down as his name passed her lips, grinning when he realized she'd been talking in her sleep. "Darren..."

He kissed the top of her head, and she raised her face. He tried to resist, knowing it wasn't right to take advantage of her fatigue. But when her lips grazed his neck, sending a shiver through his body, he was lost. He leaned down and took her mouth with his, her lips opening hungrily to accept him as he mated his tongue to hers.

He slipped his hand underneath her sweater, caressing her ribs with his fingers as he felt higher, skimming the edge of her bra. She made a small, mewling sound, and he ran his fingertips over her breast, circling her nipple as she arched up into his palm.

"Darren?"

He opened his eyes and looked down into her own, dark with passion and wide with surprise. "I'm sorry..." He started to pull his hand away. "I shouldn't have..."

"Don't stop," she whispered, grabbing his wrist and returning his hand to her breast. "I--I want this...you." She pulled his head back down to hers with her other hand, and he grinned, nipping at her lips and then placing tiny kisses along her jaw. He rolled her onto her back and worked her sweater up over her head, wishing for light to see by. He kissed her shoulders, reached behind her to unhook her bra and pulled it off. Leaning down, he pressed soft kisses all over her breast before taking the pebbled nipple into his mouth. She groaned, and he rolled his tongue over her sensitive tip as his hands worked to undo the button of her jeans and slide the zipper slowly down. He could feel the soft cotton of her panties as his fingers slid through the opening, and she gasped, her hands pulling desperately at his shirt.

He rose up to pull it off over his head, nearly going crazy when her fingers raked down his chest. He undid his jeans and pushed them off his hips as she explored lower, dipping below the waistband of his briefs. She pushed them off, and grasped his hard cock, taking him closer to the edge. He grabbed her hand and bent down for a kiss. "You need to slow down, or I'm going to be done before we get started, sweetheart," he murmured against her lips.

She moved her hands to his hips as he pulled her jeans and panties off all at once. She pulled him down over her and he buried his face between her breasts, reveling in the feel of her fingers tangling through his hair. He kissed his way down her soft, smooth belly, to the wild nest of curls guarding her innermost secrets. Suddenly the pressure on his head changed, grew more insistent as she tried to pull him up her body again.

"Are you okay?" He crawled up her body, looking into her face for any sign of what might be wrong. "Did I hurt you?"

She kissed him and then turned her face away. "No one's ever...done that before."

"Done what?" He frowned, confused. "Tell me what's wrong, sweetheart."

She raised a hand to her head, a nervous giggle falling from her lips. "Down there. No one's touched me that way before."

"You mean down here?" He slid a finger through her dense curls, circling her clit and then pressing it lightly, wringing a cry from her lips. "You mean no one's ever put his mouth on you there?" She nodded, and even in the darkness he could feel the heat on her cheeks. He grinned. "Honey, you're in for a treat. Just lay back and relax." He kissed his way back down her body, licking the apex of each of her thighs before he spread her innermost lips with his fingers. He leaned in to taste her, and she moaned, writhing under his mouth as he kissed and laved at her center. When his tongue entered her, she rose up, arching into him as her orgasm came quick, strong and hot. He suckled her until the waves subsided and kissed his way back up to her neck, rolling to his side and pulling her close.

"Oh god," she breathed, burying her face in the crook of his shoulder. "That. Was. Amazing."

He grinned, running his fingers through her hair and throwing one leg over hers. "Glad you enjoyed it. I know I did."

A little furrow appeared on her brow. "You did?"

He chuckled at her disbelief, rolling her on her back again, leaning over her. "I did," he said pressing a moist kiss to her mouth. "I love the taste of you."

"Mmm..." she pushed on his chest until he rolled off her, and she raised herself up on one elbow, circling one of his nipples with one finger. "Does this feel as good for you as it does for me?"

Electrical impulses jumped through his skin as she teased and tickled his sensitive nubs. "It's...ah..." he jumped as she switched to the other nipple. "Amazing," he gasped out, arching up into her touch. His hips bucked a little as his cock responded to her teasing, and he wondered how long he could handle her play.

"Are you ticklish?" she asked. He nodded, writhing as her fingers skittered lightly over his torso and down the sides of his ribs. The tickling sensation was eclipsed by something else, something sensual as he focused on her warm, feather-light touch. Too late, he realized she was leaning over him, her hair brushing soft against his skin. "I wonder if you taste good," she murmured just before she bent to lick a slow path across one nipple.

He jumped again, fighting the urge to cry out. His dick was so hard it was practically begging for release. She slid her hand down his belly, over one hip and around to curl her hot fingers around his shaft. He jerked up, barely able to keep from coming in her hand.

"It's okay," she whispered low in his ear. "Unless you have a condom, that is. We really can't make that mistake again."

He groaned. "Dammit." She laughed, the sound soothing his annoyance at the lack of forethought as she slowly caressed him, up and down, up and down. He moved with her, faster, showing her what tempo he needed as he climbed higher toward his own release. Just when he was almost there, she took one of his nipples in her mouth and suckled, the combined sensation sending him soaring off the edge as he climaxed hard. His seed spurted over his belly and her hand as his thrusts subsided, and he lay there focused on breathing as she gently released him and turned her back.

He wanted to ask if she was okay, but it took all of his effort just to breathe as he came down from the incredible orgasm she'd given him. He tried to move a hand, to touch her back, but didn't have the strength. When she turned back to him, and laid a cloth - his shirt, he guessed - over his softening cock, he smiled. "Thank you," he said, reaching down to clean himself up as she watched. He tossed the shirt to the side and reached for her, relieved when she came willingly into his arms.

"Are you going to call me when we get home?" Her tone was teasing, but there was an underlying hint of doubt there that he wished he could vanquish for good.

He clasped her tighter, tucking the blankets in close around them to create their own little cocoon.

"Every day," he promised, kissing her temple as she snuggled against him. "And every night too, if you'll let me."

She nodded, her breathing slow, and he closed his eyes, drifting off to sleep with her in his arms, where she was meant to be.

* * *

Marie woke the next morning to warm, male limbs wrapped tightly around her, and the spicy, somewhat musky scent of Darren enveloping her senses. She blinked, bending one arm up to rub the forearm that snaked across her chest, suddenly aware of the arousal pressing into her backside.

Heat rose in her face as she remembered last night and her wanton behavior. Had she really let him kiss her down there? And jerked him off? Suddenly afraid of what he would think of her in the light of day, she tried to wiggle out of his hold, only to have him pull her closer.

"Where are you off to so early?" The low timbre sounded deep in her ear, his warm breath against her neck sending shivers down her spine. Moisture started to pool between her legs, and she marveled that his voice was all it took to get her hot and bothered. "Running away from me again?"

She smiled, nervous as the urge to get up was suddenly very strong. "I...ah...have to go find a restroom, so to speak."

"I guess that's unavoidable." He didn't sound upset as he let her go, and she didn't dare to glance back at him as she hastily pulled her jeans on, followed by a shirt and sweatshirt. She shoved her feet into her shoes and ran out of the tent.

When she returned, he was up and dressed, his back to her as he finished rolling up her sleeping bag. He set it beside his, already rolled, and turned, a wide grin across his lips when he caught site of her. "Good morning," he said, crossing to her in just three long steps. He pulled her to him and placed a long, moist kiss on her lips that nearly took her breath away.

"Uh, good morning," she said, licking her lips and looking past him at the boxes he'd set out in front of the tables. "You've gotten a good start, I see."

He gave her a strange look, almost challenging, but she wasn't sure what it meant. Whatever it was, he quickly replaced it with his normal friendly demeanor and released her. "I thought we could get the equipment packed up first and leave your samples until last, so they'd be easily accessible when we get back. If you and Nell want to pack, Scott and I can start making trips up to the truck. We should be ready to leave by noon, I think."

She nodded. "That sounds good. I haven't seen the others yet - they must still be sleeping."

"I'll go wake them up," he said, pausing for a moment. "Are you okay? After last night, I mean..."

She couldn't look at him, and reached for an unused box of slides to hide her nerves. "Yes. Absolutely. Why wouldn't I be?" She peeked at him out of the corner of her eye, surprised to see amusement on his face. She frowned, turning to look at him. "Why are you laughing at me?"

He laughed, touching the side of her face in a caress. "You're so nervous. Every muscle in your body is tense." He took the slides out of her hand, and placed them in the box. He leaned in and kissed her again, nipping at her lips until she finally relaxed against him. "Relax," he said, pressing one last kiss on her forehead. "You have nothing to be nervous about."

"Looks like someone got a good night's sleep." Nell stood just inside the tent, a wide grin on her face. "Should I come back later?"

Marie tried to step back, but Darren held her in place. "Nope," he said, rubbing a hand lightly over Marie's arm. She wished he'd let her go - her face was burning up with embarrassment. "I was just coming out to wake you both up. We need to get moving." He finally let go, and Marie took a giant step back, nearly losing her balance and earning a laugh from Nell as Darren winked and then walked out of the tent.

"Don't worry, honey," Nell said after the tent flaps closed behind him. "Men have a talent at keeping us off balance."

Marie nodded. "You can say that again." She motioned to the tables. "We're going to pack up, and the guys will pack it out. Start wherever you'd like, but let's keep the samples on top where they'll be easy to reach when we get home."

"Will do," Nell said, grabbing a box.

Several hours later, Marie helped Nell roll up the last of the canvas. It was just after noon, and they were waiting for the guys to come back so they could take the last load out together. She looked around the valley, so quiet and peaceful, and for just a moment wished she could leave her old life and stay there forever.

"It's beautiful, isn't it?" Nell came to stand beside her, gazing out across the pond.

Marie nodded. "Yes, it is." She glanced toward the path that would take them out the way they came. "But it's time to go home," she said as Darren and Scott came into view. With one last look around, she followed Nell to meet them.

* * *

The trip home went far more smoothly than the first, and Marie found herself unlocking her office door just twelve hours after leaving the oasis. Darren had wanted to go with her, but she'd insisted that she needed some time alone to get started typing up her research. Really, she just needed some time away from him to process everything that had happened between them. He'd been beside her all the way home - in the truck, on both flights - the perfect companion. Everything just seemed to be happening too fast.

She flipped on the lights to her office and went in, setting her portfolio on the desk and collapsing into her chair. While she waited for the computer to power up, she went through her notes, numbering specific points and trying to decide how best to present her ideas. She had just opened a new document when someone knocked at her door. Riley Adams strutted in and took a seat, not waiting for an invitation.

"Have a good trip, Dr. Simco?" His arrogant smirk made her flesh crawl. He looked down at the papers on her desk, raising his eyebrows. "Getting ready to publish, are we?"

She gathered up the pages, turning them face down at her side where they were out of reach, just to be safe. "I may be," she said, not wanting to give him any more information than necessary. "My research went as well as could be expected, considering you sent someone to sabotage it." No sense in dancing around the issue, and from the frustrated look on his face, she could tell she struck a nerve.

"From what I hear, he only did half the job though. In fact, I hear he did an excellent job of seducing you, and forgot to finish stealing your work."

It took her a few minutes to process what he'd said, and after it registered, she struggled to keep her emotions hidden. "Are you admitting to trying to sabotage my work, Dr. Adams?"

He leaned forward, resting his elbows on his knees. "My condolences for the loss of your colleague. I'm sure it must have been very difficult to lose one in the field." He stared at her for a long moment while she tried to remain stoic. Then he stood and walked to the door. "Good luck, Dr. Simco. May the best scientist win."

He left and Marie forced herself to get up and close the door. She clicked the lock into place before she sat back in her chair, crossed her arms on the desk and put her head down. Darren had been working for Adams this whole time – or so Riley claimed. But he hadn't stolen her notes...in fact he'd helped her get them back. She lifted her head to look at the stack of papers that held the key to her future. They'd been in his possession long enough for him to make a copy, even if he'd handwritten them, but Adams said he hadn't gotten any information. Had Darren changed his mind? Or was Riley just lying?

She leaned back, letting her head fall against the headrest and closed her eyes. Was it worth it? Was any of this worth all the pain she'd brought on her team, and herself? Letting out a huge sigh, she gathered up her papers and put them back in her portfolio. There was still some testing to be done before she could finalize the write-up, and at the moment, she couldn't think straight enough to even know where to begin. She'd go home, get some sleep and come at it fresh in the morning. Right after she talked to Darren. This time, she was going to hear what he had to say first. She owed him that much.

* * *

Darren sat in the parking garage, one row up from where Marie's little Fiat was parked. She had wanted time alone, she said - to process everything that had happened. He'd left her at her apartment, but his instincts told him not to let her out of his sight, so he'd followed her to the lab, and waited. He wasn't sure if his old boss would try anything or not, but he'd seen the old coot's car when they pulled in. He was up to no good, that was certain.

He checked his watch - ten-fifteen. Movement near the elevators caught his eye, and Adams stepped out. But he didn't walk toward his own car. Darren watched as he walked to Marie's vehicle, and lowered himself in the space between hers and the next. Was he really planning to attack her himself?

Darren reached up to unscrew the dome light and then eased his car door open, leaving it slightly ajar as he got out. He'd take care of Adams before Marie came out. He started down the ramp and then heard the elevator ding. His heart caught in his throat as Marie started walking toward her car, her portfolio in hand.

He launched into a sprint as she drew closer to her car, and watched as Adams stood, something small, black and shiny in his hand. Marie stopped when she saw the gun, and Darren was close enough to see her face mottled with tears. She must have been crying before she came out - what had Adams done to her?

"Marie, get down," he yelled as he closed in on her. She looked at him, her eyes wide in surprise and confusion as she glanced from him to Adams. "Get down - on the ground. Now!"

She dropped to her knees just before he reached her, and he flung himself in front of her just as Adams pulled the trigger. A sharp pain shot through his side, and he winced as he hit the ground hard, right at Adams' feet.

"How nice of you to deliver yourself, Dr. Newbury. I was coming to see you next. Now I won't have to make a special trip." He lowered the gun just as Darren rolled underneath Marie's car. He flipped his pocket knife out and swiped it firmly across the back of Adams' ankle, a cry of pain confirming he'd hit his target just before the man fell to the ground. The gun flew out of Adams' hand and across the garage floor. Darren rolled out from the other side of the car and scrambled to reach it first.

Marie shot out from nowhere and grabbed the gun before either of them could get to it. She held it pointed at Adams, her hands shaking. Darren hobbled toward her, holding his side. "Good job, sweetheart - hand me the gun, and I'll hold him while you call the cops." She shook her head though, glancing quickly at him with a crazed look in her eyes.

"No. I keep the gun. You call the cops." She moved a few steps away from him, as if she didn't trust him.

Dr. Adams laughed. "I told her all about it, my boy - although it would have been nice if you'd held up your end of the deal." Darren frowned. He was starting to feel woozy, and he pressed harder on the wound in his side.

"We didn't have any deal," he said. "You crazy bastard." He looked back to Marie. Was that a glimmer of hope in her eyes? "We didn't have a deal, I swear." He stumbled back against the car, sliding down to the concrete floor. He pulled out his cell phone and dialed nine-one-one, even though he swore he heard sirens approaching below. "You have to believe me - he's lying."

He looked up at Marie, longing to reassure her, to make her see that he'd never do anything to hurt her, but he was tired. So tired. He closed his eyes. Just a quick nap and then he'd tell her he loved her.

Chapter Sixteen

Marie sat at Darren's side, the steady beep of a heart monitor droning on in the background as she waited for him to wake up. The bullet hadn't hit anything vital, but he had required surgery to remove it, and she'd been here all night with him.

He'd insisted that he hadn't made any deal with Dr. Adams, and Marie believed him. It didn't matter anymore what anyone said – she knew in her heart that he was innocent. If he would only wake up, maybe they could find the truth together.

The door opened behind her, and Marie glanced over her shoulder, expecting the nurse. Nell walked in instead. "How you holding up?"

"Okay, I guess." Marie tried to smile, though she wasn't sure she actually managed it. "How did you know we were here?"

"Emery called from the university. The lab called

him after the police and everyone left last night, and he asked me to check on you. He'll be up later today." She nodded at Darren. "How's he doing?"

Marie sighed. "The doctor said he should be waking up any time. I guess he had some sort of reaction to the anesthesia, so it's taking longer than normal." She took his hand, squeezing lightly.

Nell took the empty chair by the window. "What was that all about, anyway? I hear that when the police got there, you had a gun on Adams?"

"Yeah, I guess." Marie shook her head, still not quite believing she'd held a gun on someone. "But he pulled it on me first. He wanted my research papers. Apparently the snitch he hired didn't get the job done, so he decided to do it himself."

Nell tilted her head with interest. "He admitted to hiring Cynthia?"

Marie shook her head. "Actually, he implied that he hired Darren to seduce me and take my notes. Although he did know about Cynthia's death - how, I'm not sure."

"So there was someone else on the inside. How do you know Darren wasn't the guy?"

Marie shrugged. "I can't explain it. I just do." She looked at his face, so peaceful in sleep. "He wouldn't do that to me."

"For what it's worth, I agree with you." Nell smiled, and Marie appreciated the sentiment. "But that means someone else is out there. Since it's not me - I hope you'll take my word on that - there's only one person left."

Marie snapped her head around, realization dawning. "Scott. He was supposed to seduce me, but that didn't work so he went after Cynthia instead. But he never got the papers from her...that's what Adams meant. God, I'm so stupid."

"You're not stupid."

The raspy words had Marie turning back to look at Darren, who blinked a couple times before he could keep his eyes open. Nell came around the other side of the bed, and pressed the call button for the nurse. "Hey there - glad you could bother to wake up. We were starting to get worried."

Marie wiped a tear from her check as Darren's eyes finally locked with hers. "Welcome back," she whispered, stroking his hair back from his face. The door opened behind her and a nurse bustled in, shooing them both away from the bed so she could check his vitals.

Marie went to stand by Nell as the nurse checked Darren over. He was pale, tired and a mess, and still the most handsome man she'd ever seen.

"Looks like you're doing well," the nurse told him, catching Marie's attention. She turned to Marie. "Are you his wife?"

She shook her head. "No...I'm just--"

"My fiancé."

Marie just stared at the nurse after Darren's bold

declaration, too stunned to move or say anything else. The nurse didn't seem to notice, she just nodded and smiled. "I'll have the doctor come talk to you about his medications and such - you can probably take him home later today. He'll need someone to stay with him for twenty-four hours, but that shouldn't be a problem, will it?"

"Um, I guess not."

"Great! I'll be back in a little while then." She bounced out the door, her blond ponytail swinging as she pulled the door shut behind her.

Nell grabbed Marie's shoulders and propelled her back to the side of the bed. Darren grinned up at her. Nell might have said she'd see her later. The door opened and closed, and suddenly, Marie was alone with a man who may have just proposed.

"What, no kiss for your future husband?" His tone was teasing, but she started to sink down into the chair she'd recently vacated. He grabbed her hand with surprising strength, redirecting her to sit on the bed beside him instead. "Marie? Are you okay?" His expression grew concerned, and he rubbed soothing circles on the back of her hand with his thumb.

"I...um..." She finally blinked, the world coming back into focus. "Did you -- why did you do that?" She screwed up the courage to look into his eyes, searching for any sign that he hadn't been serious.

He winked. "Because I was hoping you'd marry me," he said, bringing her hand to his lips, and kissing her ring finger. "I know it's too soon, but..."

Marie got off the bed, pulling her hand gently away. "It is too soon," she said, pacing the tiled floor. "I can't make a decision like this when everything in my life is so upside down." She stopped, chewing on her lower lip. "I'm sorry, really I am."

"It's okay." His face fell, and he reached for her, letting his hand drop to the bed when she didn't come to him. "You need time. I understand. I won't push."

She moved back to the chair. "Thank you," she said, tentatively reaching out to squeeze his hand again. "When everything is over, maybe..."

"Absolutely." He smiled at her, tugging her closer. "Now, would you deny an almost dying man one last kiss?"

"You're not dying," she said, grinning as she leaned down, and pressed her lips against his.

* * *

When Darren woke the next morning, Marie was gone. He panicked for a moment until he saw her purse and coat on the chair.

She came out of the bathroom and the first thing he noticed were the dark, tired circles under her eyes. Guilt pricked at his conscience as he remembered asking her to stay with him last night. He shouldn't have been so selfish, he thought as she approached the bed. Then she realized he was awake, and a big smile lifted the corners of her lips as she hurried over to kiss him.

"Good morning," he said as she pulled back. She must have just brushed her teeth, and his lips tingled with the minty coolness she'd passed to him.

She grinned. "Morning. How did you sleep?" She started to reach for the chair behind her, but he tugged at her arm until she scooted up to sit beside him.

"Good, I think." He reached up, brushing her hair out of her eyes. "You look tired though - you should have gone home."

She shrugged, her gaze dropping to his chest. "I wanted to stay with you." He watched as a pretty pink blush crept into her cheeks. She was just too cute. He slid a hand around the back of her neck, pulling her down for another kiss.

Even through the weariness, she looked more peaceful than she had in days. "You don't look so worried anymore," he said, tracing a finger over her cheek.

She smiled. "Adams is under police guard in his room. He'll be arrested for attacking me when he's well enough to leave. Emery called this morning, and said the funding is mine if I want it. I told him about our find, and he seemed interested in doing more re-search into possible ways to mass produce the compounds in the Mawai plant." Her face practically glowed with excitement, and Darren couldn't help but grin back at her.

"So will you need a lab tech for this project? I happen to know one who's currently between jobs..."

She shook her head. "No. I have a team already picked out." Darren frowned. Was she worried that they couldn't work together and date? Every fiber of his being told him to fight, but he held it back. This was her decision, and she needed to know he'd support her no matter what.

"I see." He shrugged and looked out the window, surprised when she reached out and caressed his face, turning it back to hers once more. Her eyes were soft, and something told him he'd misread her.

"I don't need a *tech*," she said. "But I could use a partner on the project. Would you be interested in that?"

"Absolutely." He pulled her down until her face was just centimeters from his. "I love you, Marie." Closing the distance, he claimed her lips in a passionate kiss. He savored the way she tasted, the sweet way she moaned at his touch. "Marry me," he whispered against her lips, nipping them lightly. "Be my partner in every way."

She pulled back a little, and he knew it had been a mistake. He started to apologize, but she covered his mouth with her fingers. Then she uttered the one word that made everything okay.

"Yes."

About the Author

A full-time webmistress by day, Jamie DeBree
writes steamy, action-packed romantic suspense late
into the night. Her goal is to create the perfect blend
of sensual attraction, emotional tension and fast-
paced adventure, similar to the television crime dramas she's hopelessly addicted to.

Born in Billings Montana, she resides there with her
husband and two over-sized lap dogs. She reads in a
wide variety of genres including romance, erotica,
action/adventure, thriller, horror and literary.

For information on upcoming books, visit
jamiedebree.com.